Tell Me Your Story

Lindsey Wood

PAGE PUBLISHING, INC.
Conneaut Lake, PA

First originally published by Page Publishing 2021

ISBN 978-1-6624-4235-3 (pbk)
ISBN 978-1-6624-4236-0 (digital)

Printed in the United States of America

Tell Me Your Story

"Revolutionary War Rifle
Found at the bottom of Hackensack River"

Such simple words, yet so much more lies beneath,
more than a little plaque will ever say.

Tell me your story.
Were you a gift from father to son?
Or purchased by a young man for himself?
Your wood weathered
from years spent in that riverbed.
I suppose it was once polished,
the color revealing the exact wood you were made from,
but now the dull grayish black
only marks you as old.
Do you remember your soldier's hands
as they poured the powder and loaded the bullets?
Did they tremble
as they prepared for battle?

The metal of your trigger and barrel,
almost the same color as the wood
but not weathered and softened.
Instead, the once bright metal
is made harsh by a crusty layer of rust.
How many times
did he aim your once glinting barrel
at another soldier?
How many fell
to your leaden breath?

Your joints are weak
and nearly splitting now,
with wires serving as braces.
All your edges jagged and surfaces chipped.
Once you were a young man's source of pride
as he marched with you on his shoulder.
Even now, amid the hush of a museum
you're cocked, still waiting to fire
the shot he never got to take.
Did his cry rise above
the other sounds of war?
Or did you only realize
that he would never again pull your trigger
when you flew from limp hands
and felt the rush of the river?

Battle for the Hudson

Hugh stretched up on his toes, gripping onto the top of the earth and wood wall to pull himself up as far as he could, gaining just enough height to peer over the top of the wall and look down on the Hudson River, or as much of it as he could see through the fog rising up from the water.

"Any unwanted guests?" A voice pulled Hugh's gaze away from the water below as he lowered himself to stand normally and turned to see a young man approaching. Dark curls poked out from a woolen cap and the fringes of his hunting frock swaying in the autumn breeze as he strode along the row of canons positioned along the wall.

"All clear, John," Hugh declared. "Those redcoats know we'll blow them out of the water if they try anything!" he added as John came beside him, glancing out at the river and surrounding hills where the fog mingled with the trees. Hugh hoped he didn't have to wait a whole ten years before he was as tall as John and could see over the wall so easily.

"And I suppose you'll be here firing the canons yourself, hmm?" John replied teasingly as he leaned against the wall.

"No." A slight pout tugged at Hugh's lips. "Papa says I'm to find him straight away if there's any fighting."

"Well you can't be shirking your duties as surgeon's waiter," John said with a solemn nod. "A very important job, that is. Especially during battle."

"I guess," Hugh admitted. "But it's boring just sitting around the hospital all the time." The soldiers' tales of skirmishes and near escapes definitely made for more exciting stories than cleaning and sharpening his father's tools.

"Don't talk about being bored too loud," John chuckled, reaching over to tousle Hugh's hair. "Nobody would say no to an extra pair of hands for construction on the outer fortifications."

Hugh batted his hand away with a small laugh.

"Hugh!" A voice called out in the distance. A broad-shouldered, middle-aged man came into view across the field behind them. Instead of the Continental uniform or even the hunting clothes worn by many soldiers, a long apron sporting a number reddish brown stains covered his plain shirt and breeches.

"Speaking of getting put to work," Hugh replied with a sigh. "Over here, Papa!" He called out waving to his father.

"Dr. Morrison," John greeted the man with a nod as he made his way over the hilly ground.

Papa nodded in return. "Morning, John," he said. "Hope Hugh hasn't been any trouble."

"None, sir," John assured him with a smile. "Hugh's good company."

"In that case, sorry to part you," the doctor said, glancing over at his son. "But I'm afraid I'll be needing my waiter back," he added, placing a hand on Hugh's shoulder. "Also you should know, General Clinton's just arrived and is setting up in Fort Clinton."

"Hasn't General Clinton been here all this time?" Hugh asked glancing up between them. He knew Fort Clinton was the other fort that helped with the Hudson's defenses and was located on the southern bank of Popolopen Creek while they were in Fort Montgomery on the northern bank just where the creek fed into the Hudson River. But Brigadier General Clinton had been here at Fort Montgomery for a while now so how could he have just arrived? And why was he at the other fort?

"The other one," Papa replied with a fond smile at his son. "General *James* Clinton's here at this fort. General *George* Clinton is in command of all the forces in both forts."

"I thought he was attending to his responsibilities as governor?" John spoke up with a slight frown.

"He was, but seems he caught wind of the British planning a move against the Highlands so he thought he ought to be here. And if he's right, we'd best be on our guard."

John gave a nod, not seeming surprised that it was something serious that brought the general here. "Good thing the majority of the fortifications have been finished."

"You boys sure have been keeping busy these past months," Papa replied. "So many men have been out working I hardly see any one around the main buildings. Unless someone gets injured of course."

"Don't have to tell me," John chuckled, reaching up to massage his shoulder. "Could really use more men though. We've been managing the with building up the fortification, but if it comes to a fight for the river, we'll need a strong force."

"We'll all be hoping for reinforcements," Papa nodded with a somber look. "It's possible locals will rally with the threat so near, but our best chance is probably if Putnam can spare some troops."

"Of course, we'll get more men," Hugh piped up. "Everyone says controlling the river's the key to winning the war, right? And we're the ones protecting it."

"We're one of the first defenses to be sure," Papa replied. "But if it comes to a fight for the river, the boys'll be needing to be in top condition. Which means…" he trailed off, giving Hugh an expectant look.

"Which means back to chores," Hugh sighed at the familiar reminder.

"Right you are. Check that the supplies and tools are in good condition, and I've got a new batch of cloth. Cut what you can into bandage strips and get lint from the scraps."

"Yes, Papa," Hugh replied. "See you later, John," he added with a wave at the older boy.

John smiled and gave a nod in return before heading off to find the captain. Meanwhile, Hugh and his father made their way across the fort toward some of the earliest buildings that had been finished. They passed by the magazine, necessary, and into the midst of various barracks. Inside one was the space designated for the Morrisons' use, and most importantly, the hospital.

Some cots were laid out on one end of the room while a simple wooden table, stool, and some boxes and trunks occupied the other. Most of the cots were thankfully empty save for one with a soldier that had taken a bad fall carrying a log to be cut and had hurt his ankle a few days ago. Papa made his way over to the soldier, carefully undoing the bandages to check on his condition. Hugh dug out a pair of scissors from his father's box of supplies and started on his own task. He had helped his father prepare bandages enough to easily judge useable lengths and widths of the cloth to bind various types of wounds.

Hugh had laid out a few neat stacks of fresh bandages soon enough and then moved on to making lint for the bandage padding. He took a scrap of cloth from the pile of bits that were too small to use, laying it flat on the worktable. He took a knife and began scraping along loose threads that made up the frayed edge of the cloth. Slowly but surely tiny wisps of fuzzy lint came off, and Hugh carefully gathered them up between his fingers and put it away in a box with the rest of the lint supply when a shadow crossed the threshold of the door. Hugh glanced up to see the figure of a man in the doorway. He wore a well-kept uniform, and even in the partial light, the boy recognized the barrel-chested figure and neatly queued hair of Brigadier General James Clinton.

"Dr. Morrison?" he said. The general stepped inside the doorway, and another figure appeared close behind. The second man was also dressed in a fine uniform, and though he looked a few years younger than General Clinton, as he turned his head to take in the room, the silhouette of his prominent nose was a close enough match to the general's that they had to be brothers.

"Right with you, sir," the doctor replied glancing over briefly before returning his attention to his patient. "It's quite a bruise to be sure but definitely nothing broken, and the gashes seem to be healing all right, no sign of infection. We'll get it rewrapped just to be safe, but then you can return to your barracks. Take it easy for another day or two, and you'll be good as new." He stood, glancing over his shoulder toward Hugh. "Hugh, wrap up his ankle for me, just like last time."

"Yes, Papa." Hugh obediently picked up the bit of lint he had managed and put it in the box before setting the knife aside and going over to the soldier's cot and began wrapping the strip of cloth around the soldiers ankle, remembering what Papa told him about not making it too tight or too loose.

With that taken care of, Papa made his way over to the general with a respectful nod of his head. "What can I do for you, general?" he asked, pausing a moment as he noticed the second man. "Ah, generals?" he corrected, glancing between the two of them.

"Doctor, I'd like you to meet my brother. Governor of New York and commander here, Brigadier General Clinton," the general replied, gesturing to the man beside him.

"George, this is our surgeon, Dr. Robert Morrison," he added before turning his attention back to Papa. "He wanted to be properly updated about the situation here and so wanted to talk with you, if you have the time."

"Certainly," Papa replied with a nod. "An honor to meet you, sir," Papa replied with a polite bow of his head.

General Clinton nodded before taking his leave, letting his brother and Papa talk together. Most likely, he had drills and aspects of the constructions still to attend to. Neither seemed to notice that Hugh had finished wrapping the soldier's leg; if the man himself even noticed, he said nothing. Both were caught up in their own curiosity, remaining in place to listen to the doctor and general speak.

"Is there anything particular you wanted to know?"

"I'd like to make sure we're as prepared as we can be," he replied. "How has the men's conditions been?"

"Mercifully, we've not had too many contagions crop up," Papa replied. "Most of my patients have been injuries from construction mishaps or minor skirmishes."

"I'm glad to hear it," Clinton replied. "It's ready soldiers we're most in need of. We'll need every one we can get soon enough."

"Well, I'll be doing my best to keep them hale and hearty, general," Papa promised with a somber nod.

"Your work is much appreciated Doctor. I trust you have everything you need to do so?"

Papa nodded. "Well enough to manage. The quartermaster knows what sort of supplies I need most often and does his best to send them my way when he can. We'll all have to learn to make a little go a long way before the end of this war."

"That we will," General Clinton replied. "Just creating these fortifications has been no small feat and the work of holding the river is only just begun. But I won't take up any more of your time unless there's anything else I should be aware of."

"I can't think of much of anything else to report as far as the hospital is concerned," Papa replied. "Fortunately, all has been going as well as can be expected."

"No news is good news in this regard. Keep up the good work, doctor," the general replied before glancing over at Hugh and the solider on the cot. "And I hope your recovery continues, soldier."

"Yes, sir," Papa said before General Clinton made his way out the door as the soldier nodded.

As he left, Papa came over to the soldier, bending to check Hugh's work on the bandaging. He gave an approving smile at Hugh before looking back to the patient. "That should do it. Like I said, don't be exerting yourself too much, but just walking and getting some exercise will be fine."

"Thank you, Doctor Morrison," he replied with a grateful nod before rising and gingerly making his way out of the hospital.

Hugh watched him go, the conversation between his father and General Clinton still on his mind. "Papa." He glanced up, his head tilted slightly. "I thought yesterday you said you'd like some camphor and laudanum," he said. Papa knew how to make a number of poultices and infusions, but some treatments needed imported ingredients or were complicated to prepare. At home, he would tell patients to go to the town's apothecary for those, but out in the fort, they were harder to come by.

"I did," Papa nodded. "If it comes to a battle, quite a few men will likely be severely injured and only a matter of time before sickness spreads. I'd prefer to tend such things with properly made medicine if I can."

"So why didn't you tell the general that?"

Papa crossed the room to sit on the stool where Hugh had been working on the lint earlier, gesturing for Hugh to follow. "The army is well-aware of what a surgeon generally needs, and I keep the quartermaster informed of what I'm using or getting low on, there's no need to trouble the general with it when he no doubt has plenty else on his mind."

"But couldn't he order that you be given more money or things you need, especially since he's the governor too?" Hugh asked.

"General Clinton might be in charge of things here but most of our funds come from elsewhere," Papa replied with a small smile. "He can't make money or supplies appear out of thin air."

"Well then, he could ask…General Washington. Or Congress," Hugh persisted, remembering the names that usually came up when soldiers talked about the main authorities in the army.

Papa sighed, resting a hand on Hugh's shoulder. "Perhaps if there were funds to spare," he said, his somber tone drawing Hugh's gaze up to look at him. "But you have to understand, this war is a big effort, Hugh. The Hudson's important, certainly, but there's other fronts up north and even in other colonies. There's a great deal at stake, and the fact is every penny we have needs to be spent carefully. Do you remember what I said when you and I set out for the fort?"

"That every man has to do his part to protect our rights," Hugh echoed, remembering the day he and his father had left home.

"Exactly, these men," Papa said, gesturing out the door to the fort beyond, "they've left their homes and faced hardships because they want to stand up to the crown's tyranny just like us. They're risking their lives to defend our homes and our families from the British and Tory neighbors."

Hugh frowned. He knew Tories were people that were still loyal to the crown. He had heard people in town last year saying that Tories would gladly see anyone fighting for their freedom hanged as rebels.

"So if we're to help them do that, yes, I need certain things to keep the soldiers healthy and able to go on, but that comes after they've faced the greatest dangers. I can't heal men who've starved before the fight even begins or don't make it off the field because they ran out of powder to cover a retreat. If these men are to have any chance of holding the river—of winning this war, their needs have to come first. So I can make do with what we have if it means more funds and resources to keep them fed, with shoes on their feet when the snow starts and weapons in their hands."

"I guess that makes sense," Hugh replied as he considered the idea. He thought about John and the other soldiers out working on the fortifications and preparing to defend the river. The idea of being here, seeing his friends and neighbors teach the redcoats and Tories a lesson seemed exciting, but now his father painted a somewhat different picture. "Papa," he said. "We are gonna win though, right?"

His father gave his shoulder a small squeeze, offering a smile, though Hugh recognized a hint of seriousness still in his eyes. "I won't lie to you, lad, you agreed to come and help me here which means you're going learn what war is. The odds are not in our favor, but we're fighting for our rights, for what we believe in, and our very homes and livelihoods. It's going to come at a high price no matter what, but so long as we all hold on to a bit of faith and do our part, I believe we can do something great."

"Costs?" Hugh echoed with a small frown.

Papa nodded. "Brave men have already died for the cause throughout the colonies. You've heard talk of the battles, in Massachusetts when all this started and the Canada campaign. And it's moved to New York, not just around the city but up north in Ticonderoga too."

Hugh thought of John and the other soldiers, the men who told stories around fires as they let their ashcakes bake. And the young drummers who sometimes let him play on their instruments; they weren't much older than Hugh himself. Would they make it through the war? "Does that mean men might die here?"

"I pray every night that we will be spared that," Papa assured him. "And I've vowed to do everything in my power to help anyone that is injured defending these forts. Beyond that, each of us can only do our best to serve the cause and help end the war."

"Then I'm going to enlist as soon as I'm big enough and then I can fight for the cause too," Hugh said with a resolute nod.

"It'll be a good few years before then," Papa chuckled, reaching out to tousle Hugh's hair. "And in the meantime, you can do a great deal of good by making sure there's a good supply of lint and bandaging," he added, rising from the stool and gesturing for Hugh to return to his chore.

"I'll make loads of it then!" Hugh replied, taking up the knife again and scraping it against the edge of the cloth.

"Just remember quality over quantity," Papa warned. He had told Hugh about the trouble even a bit of thread mixed in with the fuzzy lint could do if it was put on an open wound. And it seemed especially important knowing he might need to be bandaging men's wounds in a hurry if it did come to a battle.

"Yes, Papa," Hugh nodded before returning to his work, carefully picking up the pinch worth of lint that he had scraped off and placing it in the little wooden box with the rest of what he'd made before. He continued to think on what his father told him as he worked at the repetitive task. Hugh did not want to imagine losing any of the friends he had made here at Fort Ticonderoga, but battles were dangerous things. So he would just have to put in some extra effort to really make sure they had everything they needed.

* * *

The fog returned even thicker the following morning and rose up from the river reaching toward the fort itself. Outside its walls, white mist spread through the woods, making Hugh's morning task of collecting kindling just a little harder. Not that he really minded, he could still see well enough around him, and he knew his way. As he made his way along the deer trails gathering any twigs or small branches he came across, it was mostly quiet, save for the crinkle of autumn leaves beneath his feet and distant chirping of birds. Hugh had managed to gather up a small armful of kindling when he heard hurried footsteps in the distance.

Hugh frowned, turning toward the source of the sounds. There were often others out in the woods; with autumn setting in, everyone wanted to be well-stocked on firewood, and of course, lumber was needed to build up the fortifications and the construction itself. So there was almost always some activity along the walls of the fort and out in the woods surrounding it. But this was definitely coming from further out in the woods. And it was drawing closer, but the fog combined with trees and bushes made it hard to see very far.

Soon enough, his questions were answered however as he spotted three men. Two wore the familiar brown coats with blue facings of the Fifth New York Regiment while the third wore a linen hunting frock. He vaguely recognized them as men he had seen from time to time, warming themselves by a fire or digging redoubts. But whatever relief that recognition might have brought was snatched away as they spotted him.

"Quick, back to the fort!" one of the uniformed men shouted. The one in the hunting frock did not even give Hugh a chance to follow the order as they neared where he stood. He grasped Hugh's arm and started pulling him along in the direction of the fort, spilling the twigs in his arms.

"What's the matter?" Hugh asked, the man released his arm once he managed to fall in step with them.

"British," the soldier replied. "We spotted 'em coming up from the river—fog helped 'em get in real close."

The British soldiers were here! Papa's words from yesterday echoed in Hugh's mind. The time when the men he had spent his time talking with, listening to funny stories, and helping with chores were going to have to face the British army in battle. They quickly returned to the fortifications, and the scouts wasted no time reporting what they had seen and raising the alarm. Meanwhile, Hugh dashed straight for the infirmary.

"They're here, Papa! They're attacking!" he shouted, bursting in through the door.

Papa quickly rose to his feet from where he sat at his desk, clearly surprised by his son's sudden arrival. "Hugh, what do you mean running around shouting like that here?" he scolded, but his expression seemed to soften into confusion as he took in Hugh's frightened expression.

"The British!" Hugh panted, the sprint to the fort taking its toll on him. "The scouts just saw them approaching. They're going to attack the fort!"

Papa's eyes widened as he turned toward the door where raised voices and men running with muskets in hand confirmed Hugh's words. "Quick lad, get some bandages at the ready," he instructed as he rushed to roll out his tools on the table.

"We'll fight them off, won't we, Papa?" Hugh asked as he laid out the bandages in places they would be easy to grab and use quickly.

"The fortifications will be tested, that's for sure," Papa replied as he arranged everything he anticipated to need. "Hopefully, General Putnam will be able to get a few men over here. That's what we need most of," he added under his breath.

"They'll be time for him to send them, won't there?" Hugh asked. "The redcoats don't know the best ways through the woods."

"They might not, but it won't just be them," Papa said, not even bothering to look up from his work. "They'll probably have gotten Tories to help them get the lay of the land. Might even be some of the Loyalist regiments alongside the British."

Hugh had heard about Tories forming their own regiments, some even led by wealthy landowners from the Hudson Valley itself. They would know their way around the valley and mountains just as well as many of the men here in Fort Montgomery.

Just then, a few of the women who lived in the fort hurried in carrying pitchers of water and washcloths. Papa called out orders as he and the camp followers rushed and scrambled to prepare while outside other voices raised in command and drumbeats sounded calling the men into positions. Gunfire had broken out, too, the loud bangs echoing through the woods and hillside though it sounded too distant to be at the walls of the fort yet.

"Everything's in place, Papa," Hugh spoke once he had arranged everything he could think of while the others continued their own work.

"We're going to need more water," Papa replied, looking over the pitcher's the camp followers had brought. "Quick, go and fetch another bucket."

Hugh hurried to obey, grabbing one of the wooden buckets outside the building and running across the grounds to fill the bucket and hurrying back, as fast as he could while still being careful not to spill the bucket's contents. He was just passing by the edge of the fort when suddenly the sounds of gunfire stopped. Hugh paused, caught up in the stillness that fell over the soldiers, all poised at the walls of the fort. They held their rifles at the ready, but no one fired. A few leaned over to their neighbors murmuring quietly. Out of curiosity Hugh set down the bucket and edged a little closer, spotting John he came to his side.

"Hugh?" the soldier hissed. "You should be in the barracks with your father."

"Fetching water," Hugh replied, pointing over at the bucket. "What's happened?"

"They sent out a flag of truce," John replied, turning forward again to watch. Hugh went up on his tiptoes to get a look. A man in a bright red uniform with buttons that glinted in the sunlight stood with one of Fort Montgomery's officers whose back was to them.

"Could they not have expected the fort to be ready and changed their minds about attacking?" Hugh asked in confusion as he watched the two men talking.

A man standing beside John snorted. "If only," he muttered. "More likely hoping to convince us to surrender."

Hugh scowled at the idea. "We won't do that, though?"

"Course not," John replied, shaking his head. "Our man'll hear them out for respect of the rules of war, but we're not giving up the river without a fight. Which means," he added turning away from the scene beyond the wall to face Hugh properly. "We're going to need your father before the day's out, so if he needs water, go and get it to him, quick. The front line's no place for a surgeon's waiter." Just then Hugh's attention was drawn back to the two officers. Theirs turned sharply on his heel and returned to the fort while the red-coat frowned, clearly displeased with whatever had been said before returning to his own lines.

"Fair treatment if we surrender," one of the soldiers scoffed as word of the conversation passed down the line. "Fair to hand over all our rights to a tyrant."

"Well, they can have the same promise if they decide to surrender," another replied, moving his rifle into position as he awaited the orders.

"I mean it now, Hugh. Get on back to your father," John spoke up, reaching a hand to Hugh's shoulder and gently but firmly turning him around to head back.

"I'm going, I'm going," Hugh assured, returning to his bucket and continuing on his way. Soon enough, he could hear shouted commands to fire, and the guns and canons boomed once again.

The infirmary was still bustling with activity when Hugh arrived as everyone rushed to prepare anything they could think of. He had no sooner stepped inside the door and set the bucket down against the wall than one of the women swept it up, and Papa had a new task for him.

"Hugh, did you manage to fill the lint box from yesterday's cloth?" he called across the room.

"Not quite," Hugh admitted. He had worked for hours to get a good amount, but he remembered there still being some space left.

"Here you are, lad," one of the women said, pushing a few worn-out kerchiefs and what looked like mending scraps into his hand. "Can never have too much lint, especially having to conserve the comfrey and soapwort as much as we can." The herbs were useful for healing and made into a poultice could serve as enough of a cushioning without lint. But in October, they had only dried herbs to work with that would have to last them all through any future battles or accidents until the spring.

Hugh took the bits of cloth and brought them over to his father's portable writing desk, placing it on a stool beside the window. They would need the table for tools and possibly even men if the beds got filled up, but the tiny, slanted box would serve no good for that, and Papa would not have time to sit still by any patient's bedside once they started coming. But the writing desk was fine for scraping the lint, and the stool brought it to just the right height for sunlight to make it easy to see the lint coming off. The gunfire grew louder as Hugh worked steadily, adding in pinches of lint to the wooden box as quickly as he could.

Soon men were filtering in, some stumbling on their own while others had to be supported by others bringing them in. And Hugh knew that these were probably only a small sample of the men who were injured. These were men whose injuries prevented them from continuing the fight, arms hanging limply at their side or hands broken and shattered or near unconscious as they were half dragged in by camp followers who had been delivering water for the canons or doing other tasks when they saw the men fall. Anyone who was injured but still capable of lifting a rifle would press on. Hugh even wondered if there might be injured men who had collapsed and just went unnoticed amid the shouted orders and smoke-filled air. Hugh could already catch a hint of gunpowder carried on the breeze through the door and windows.

Hugh had seen bad injuries before; neighbors called on Dr. Morrison's help when they cut themselves with a scythe while harvesting wheat or all sorts of broken bones. Even some of the accidents that happened while the soldiers built the fort had been bloody and messy. He had learned to be a good assistant, to just not look too closely at injuries beyond getting an idea of what his father might need. But now, he found himself wondering what battle wounds would look like. How many men would be wounded in this battle and would they be able to help all of them?

With those worries in mind, Hugh set to his task with even more determination. One thing was for sure, even if not every soldier could be treated, it wouldn't be for a lack of bandaging supplies. Whenever he came to a larger piece of cloth, he cut it to strips that could be used as bandages before scraping at the leftover shreds for lint. As more and more of the other supplies were set up, some of the women and their children also joined him, diligently scraping over the bits of cloth, only stopping to help guide new patients in or assist treating an urgent injury.

Outside the building seemed to have erupted into chaos. There was shouting and screams and volley after volley sounding. Smoke drifted over the hilly ground from explosions that Hugh was sure seemed to be coming closer. A few times, he thought he even felt the ground shake.

"How long until Putnam's reinforcements reach us?" one of the women asked.

"Who knows," another replied, her expression set in a grim frown. "There's no telling if he'll even send them. There's Fort Clinton and possibly other points to be defended as well."

"But he—" Hugh broke off as a particularly loud explosion echoed over the fort. "But he has to send us help—no one wants to lose the river."

"We can hope, lad," the second woman replied. "But he's got to weigh a lot of things, some we may not even know about."

He supposed she was right. Fort Clinton was just a short distance from here so it made sense the British would have come prepared to fight both forts. Suddenly, there were shouts of panic and officers' voices valiantly trying to issue orders above it all. Though canons still boomed somewhere in the distance, the sounds of rifles firing now mixed with shouts and cries of pain as hand-to-hand fighting began. The explosions and booms seemed to shake the ground and make the walls rattle all around them. Hugh did his best to ignore the sounds, not thinking about what the soldiers like John and his other friends might be facing, or the chilling screams that came from outside.

That was until pain tore across Hugh's forehead, and he belated realized the latest scream was his own. He hit the floor of the infirmary hard, his vision seeming to blur as he lay there too stunned to even realize what happened. His head hurt, and there was something warm and sticky when he brought his hand to touch it. Whatever it was it was dripping down too, sticking to his eyelashes.

"Dr. Morrison, come quick!" a woman's voice shouted in fright. Hugh felt hands hastily moving to pick him up, steadying him upright. Hugh blinked his eyes open to see a woman kneeling in front of him. One hand remained in place helping Hugh to stay standing on his trembling legs while the other lifted a corner of her apron to wipe at Hugh's face. "Good heavens child," she murmured.

"I…I…" Hugh broke off with a sniff, hoping her fussing would disguise the water building in his eyes as his voice shook.

"Hush, now, we'll have you looked after," she replied, dropping the apron Hugh finally registered the large red stain now all over the corner. The warm stuff dripping in his eyes was blood, *his* blood.

Then Papa appeared at his side, he had his little leather case of tools in hand. Immediately, Hugh lunged forward.

"Papa!" he gasped, throwing himself into his papa's arms.

"A musket ball, right through the window," the woman spoke somewhere over Hugh's head. "Of all the ill luck."

"Here now, let's have a look," Papa said, and though he spoke in what Hugh liked to call his doctor voice, the eight-year-old couldn't be sure if he imagined it or not, but he thought he heard a slight tremble. Gently, Papa moved him back a little, his fingers moving around Hugh's forehead. He pushed aside locks of hair, causing Hugh to wince a little when his fingers met a sensitive spot. "Not too deep," he murmured. "We'll want to stop the bleeding, but should heal up all right."

He reached over to gather up some of the lint Hugh had been scraping as the woman held out a long bandage. Papa moved automatically, gently laying clumps of lint over the wound and then wrapping the bandaging around Hugh's head.

"There you are," he said as he finished tying the bandage.

Hugh sniffed and hastily wiped at his eyes as Papa gave his shoulder a squeeze. "Got your first battle wound already," he said with a reassuring look. "Feel all right?"

"I...I guess so," Hugh sniffed, his voice strained and vision a little blurry with moisture. "Still hurts," he added, wiping his nose on his sleeve before reaching up to touch the bandages.

"Leave it be," Papa said, gently guiding Hugh's hand back down. "The bandaging will do its job without you poking at it."

"Doctor," one of the women spoke up. Hugh glanced over to see her guiding in a soldier. His right arm was clearly in bad shape, most of the sleeve stained red already.

"Speaking of jobs, we've got our own to do," Papa said, giving another pat on Hugh's shoulder. "You get back to the lint—away from the window this time, though."

"Y-yes, Papa," Hugh replied with another sniff, trying to ignore the tightness in his throat.

"Good lad," Papa replied approvingly before rising to stand and hurrying over to the injured soldier. Hugh gathered up the writing desk and carried it over to the wall farthest from the widows. Given how his legs shook, he decided it would be better to sit down to work from now on. Placing the writing desk on the ground, he sat on the floor beside it and set back to work. It was harder to see the lint without the sunlight, but Hugh was practiced enough to know how to get the most amount of lint at once and judge when to move on to another spot.

A couple of other soldiers staggered into the hospital, most with injuries that made it nearly impossible to use a musket or any other tasks in fighting. The number was impossibly small, however, considering the number of crashes and screams from outside. The sounds of battle were definitely getting closer.

"Fall back!" A voice carried over the chaos of the battle as drums beat out the order as well. Hugh could feel his heart pounding in his chest as he wondered what that meant. Had the British made it past the outer defenses? Could they actually be inside the fort? Hugh's hands worked faster, determined to get as much lint as possible. Papa was going to need a lot of it by the time the battle ended. Especially as it was quickly being used already, with Papa and the camp followers tending to the scattered soldiers appearing at the door.

He tried to ignore the ache in his head beneath his own bandaging, though the deafening booms of canon and gunfire were not helping. It felt like the walls shook with every explosion, and Hugh heard the sounds of stone and logs cracking mixing with shouts and screams as cannonballs found their marks. It continued on until suddenly Hugh noticed more and more men rushing past the door. Voices all around became more panicked, more frantic.

A soldier appeared in the doorway, he was out of breath and seemed a little disheveled but not particularly injured.

"We-we're in retreat!" he panted. "They've taken it, get out!"

The hospital erupted into new chaos as the word *retreat* registered, not just from the man but from other voices outside as well.

Anyone who could even hobble pushed themselves up and staggered for the door. The camp followers, too, moved to flee, some helping injured soldiers out up from their cots.

"Hugh, come on. You heard him!" Papa was by Hugh's side in an instant and pulling him up from the floor. "Get going, out of the fort, and to the river quick."

"But the lint," Hugh said, looking at the box as it slid down the tilted surface of the desk and onto the floor.

"We'll make more. Come along," Papa replied firmly ushering Hugh toward the door. They emerged out of the infirmary and into a mad rush of people and shouting. Hugh tried to look around for John or any of his other friends, but everyone was going so fast, and Papa was soon urging him along with the crowd. He held onto Papa's hand as best he could as they hurried along with the retreating soldiers.

They had made it some distance from the infirmary with what seemed like more and more soldiers, camp followers, and everyone in the fort crowding around them. Hugh's hand was sweating, and Papa was trying to pull him along as quickly as possible, but it was hard for Hugh to match his stride. Soon, the crowd was all pressing in around him, Hugh felt dizzy and out of breath, and slowly, painfully slowly, his hand was slipping out of Papa's.

He felt Papa try to readjust his grip, but Hugh had already fallen too far behind, the shift in grip was all it took for their hands to slip apart.

"Hugh!" he heard Papa's voice call out.

"Coming, Papa!" he replied, trying to pick up his pace, keeping Papa in view. But there were so many people. Everyone shouting and jostling, and Hugh was sure he had never run this hard before. Why did everyone have to be so tall? It only took a few seconds of being separated before Hugh felt lost in a sea of boots and coat hems. All he could see was the mixed uniformed shoulders above him, and Papa was nowhere to be seen.

Hugh slowed, stricken with panic at the realization they had been separated. But people rushed along, some even urging Hugh on, calling to him to keep moving or even briefly tugging him in the right direction only for him to lose track of them too. He did, however, manage to keep on his feet and keep moving, which seemed to be more than others. As he ran along, he could see figures lying motionless on the ground. Some of the ones he passed near showed signs of injury from canons or debris from nearby buildings that were hit.

If he stayed here would Papa come back? No, he'd never be able to trace his steps back in this mad rush. All around him, men lay motionless among churned up patches of grass or mud. Although there were others all scattered around him making their own mad dashes to safety, he was frightened. He wanted Papa here beside him. Hugh glanced around desperately searching for some clue of what direction Papa might be. The sight that met him instead was something else entirely though.

The fleeing crowd of soldiers had thinned around him as he fell further behind, and some soldiers decided to go different directions instead. Hugh continued to glance around, even looking back trying to find Papa or even just a more familiar face. But he quickly regretted it as he spotted more soldiers wearing neither the blues or frocks of the New York regiments. They wore red and green jackets, even after the exertion of running all this way and a few scattered stains the uniforms, all seemed neat and well-maintained. Hugh's blood ran cold as he realized the British really were here; they really were taking the fort. And worse yet, they charged with bayonets held at the ready, mercilessly slashing and stabbing at anyone they could reach. Even at the men already lying on the ground. Hugh could see them reaching up, voices calling out pleadingly for quarter, only to be quickly silenced.

Hugh had to run. He spun around on his heel and tore forward with renewed energy as he heard the screams behind echoing in his mind. *Keep going. Don't stop,* he told himself. All the while sending up a silent prayer that Papa hadn't been caught back there. The renewed adrenaline from his fear and shock sent him dashing forward, catching up with the main crowd of retreating soldiers.

Too frightened to really know where to go he simply followed where most of the soldiers seemed to be headed. Soon enough, they had fled from the fort itself, and Hugh realized they were headed in the direction of the river. He ran down the sloping hills and rocks, stumbling every so often but determined to keep going and stay on his feet. Up ahead, he could see a few small boats in the river. They had been around the shore to be used for transports; however, the retreating soldiers had quickly filled them, cramming in as many men as the boats would carry. Hugh wondered if any would brave coming back to this side to let others cross. Even if they did, would they even get back in time?

Also in the water, further along the river, was a larger ship, one Hugh had seen many times while looking out over the river. It bore the same name as the fort, *The Montgomery*. Cannonballs shot out from the ship, hissing through the air over Hugh's head and toward the British as they chased the retreating Patriots. Hugh hoped it would slow the British down, but there was still no time to waste. Especially not when he noticed more sails appearing from downriver. The southern part of the Hudson was controlled by the British, meaning those ships would be coming to help the attack.

He paused for only a moment, eyeing the river nervously; he glanced at some of the other soldiers. Some went on into the water while others stopped at the shallows hesitating, probably never having swum before. Hugh had learned to swim, even in moving waters, but nothing like the Hudson itself, and he was frightened. But the thought of those terrible screams and the sight of those bloodied bayonets scared him even more. So he gathered his courage and ran a little along the shore to where the great big chain was fastened in place. Once he found the spot where the chain stretched into the water Hugh followed the other soldiers into the river.

He felt his breath hitch a little as the bitterly cold water splashed up as he ran full speed until he was waist deep. He had to keep going so he did his best to brace himself for more cold before he lunged forward to swim on, doing his best to stay near the chain. He tried to keep his head above water, but the waves were powerful, splashing up around him. Soon, he was completely soaked, frigid water seeping into his bandages and dripping from his hair into his eyes. He could just make out the shapes of soldiers swimming up ahead before he was splashed again, blurring his vision. Hugh gulped in breaths as often as he could, just telling himself to keep going. He could hear voices calling and the sounds of canons and explosions, but just fighting the current and keeping his head up was all he could afford to focus on.

As he neared the middle of the river, the rapids grew harsher. He had swum a few times, usually in streams and smaller offshoots of the river not far from his home. But that was in summer when the cool water was a relief, not in October when the fall chill was already in the air and the water seemed even colder, and never so far out. As water surged around him, he was pushed beneath the surface and sent tumbling through the water. By luck, he felt the rough iron chain link against his hand. Limbs flailing as he tried to try to fight the current, Hugh reached out to grab at the chain through the murky water. He held on tight, terrified of being carried away by the current. But as he already could feel the strain in his lungs, he knew he had to move. So he kicked off from the chain and did his best to try and stay along its track. Breaking through the surface, he coughed and sputtered. Wiping wet hair from his eyes he glanced around, spotting the other side of the shore.

Breathing heavily, it was hard not to keep swallowing water, but he did his best to spit it out and keep moving. Occasionally, he was dipped under the water again but managed to stay near enough the chain to keep his bearings. The seconds seemed to stretch on forever as he fought the current, his clothes heavy, and what had been a dull ache from his head wound was now throbbing. The bandage was thoroughly soaked making it shift and irritate the cut. But finally, he reached the eastern shallows, his feet kicking into rock and sandy shore before he began to stumble forward, sloshing through the water. Once he reached dry land, he collapsed onto his stomach, coughing up some of the water he had swallowed. He knew he should keep moving; lying on the banks of the river would not be safe for long. But after that swim his arms and legs felt like jelly, and it was all he could do to try and get his burning lungs to work right.

The sounds of battle could still be heard from across the water as the moments passed. But Hugh did not even lift his head to see, his mind screaming to move but his limbs too exhausted to do so. That was until the sound of a familiar voice broke through the sounds of everyone making their own escapes and canons booming.

"Hugh!"

He turned his head at the sound of his name to see John rushing along the banks toward him. "You're all right," he said, panting from running but still sounding relieved. "Where's Dr. Morrison?"

"We…we g-got separated…I—I don't…he was there and…" Hugh said, his voice trembling as he pushed the words out through chattering teeth. Hugh slowly pushed himself up and rolled over, propping himself up on his elbows. The reminder and renewed worry about Papa helping him ignore the way his arms shook just from that small exertion.

"I'm sure he'll make his way here, it'll be all right," John replied. "We—" He was cut off by a deafening boom that Hugh swore he could *feel* in the ground and the air itself. Both boys' gaze shot toward the fort to see a dark shape shoot up into the air, thrown by the force of a pillar of flame beneath it.

"The magazine…" John's voice was little more than a stunned whisper. The flames slowly faded, shrinking to just a slight glow; however, dark trails of smoke continued to rise up from the fort in the distance.

"What happened?" Hugh asked, looking from the smoke to John.

"Must've put a torch to the magazine," he explained. "Least we know the walls stood strong."

The magazine. That was where all the gunpowder was stored. Hugh remembered hearing about how important it was to build that particular structure. The men had been determined to make the walls as solid and sturdy as possible. Of course, there were rules about being sure to avoid unnecessary fire or sparks anywhere near the building, but everyone had been determined to make the walls hold strong even if there was a mishap. And as a result, apparently the only direction the explosion had been able to go was upward.

"But…all the powder…they destroyed it all?" Hugh asked, dumbfounded at the idea. Powder was always so carefully used, everyone wanting to be sure there was enough of it.

"Colonial powder's not even worth stealing to them," John replied, a note of bitterness in his voice. He spared little time for his shock and indignation, however, and was quickly pulling Hugh to his feet.

"They're destroying everything," Hugh whispered, staring wide-eyed up at the fort as more smoke rose from different parts. As if the destruction of Fort Montgomery wasn't bad enough, on the hill beside it, he could see the neighboring Fort Clinton was under just as fierce an attack. The smoke and flames were not quite so far along as Fort Montgomery's, but there were a few of them, and flashes and echoing booms coming from it suggested it would soon be in much the same state as its neighbor.

"Come on," John urged, pulling Hugh away from the river. The younger boy followed him some ways into the woods but soon fell behind, stumbling on the leaf-strewn ground and his breathing still coming ragged. Still, he knew they had to keep moving. The British probably wouldn't cross the river right away, but it seemed best to get as much distance between them as possible.

Eventually though, it was just too much. Exhaustion left him far less surefooted then he usually was, and he caught a tree root wrong. Hugh pitched forward just managing to break his fall and landing on his hands and knees. Hearing him fall, John stopped, turning back and hurrying to Hugh's side.

"You all right?" he asked, reaching out to help Hugh up.

Hugh only managed to move into a sitting position. "Tired," he panted.

John sighed, glancing around and seeming to consider their options for a moment. Though he was better off than Hugh, he was still breathing heavily and sporting a few scrapes and tears in his clothes.

"Here," he said, crouching down with his back to Hugh. "Climb on, we can rest when we've gotten a little further."

Hugh wrapped his arms over John's shoulders and held on as the older boy slipped his arms securely beneath Hugh's legs and rose to stand. "How's your head?" John asked as they continued on through the woods.

"Stings a little," Hugh admitted, having to resist the temptation to reach up and touch the bandages. He could feel they were slipping a little after the swim but seemed to be mostly in place. "Papa wrapped it."

"That'll explain how the bandages held on after the river," John replied. "Dr. Morrison knows his trade."

"Back in the fort...I tried to stay with him," Hugh spoke up hesitantly. "But everyone was running...Do you think...he made it out?" Hugh asked.

John did not answer right away, instead continuing to press on through the underbrush. "There were a lot of men crossing the river," he said after a few moments. "And I don't think there was any assault on the north side, your father could've made it either way."

"I should've stuck closer to him." Hugh said, his voice quiet as his stomach felt like it was tying itself in knots. "The men that fell behind...They were..." he trailed off, remembering the men being killed.

"I know," John replied, his tone somber. "But he might have made it out. Even if you got separated, he was probably not too far from you—just lost in the crowd."

"I guess so," Hugh replied, trying to hold on to some hope that John was right. Papa was smart and knew his way around the fort so he could have made his way out safely. Though a part of Hugh could not help thinking about how his Papa wouldn't like passing by wounded men without trying to help them. But he had to hope for the best. Once they were safe, he could work on figuring out how to get home or maybe even find Papa.

The conversation faded, the sounds of John's somewhat heavy breathing and distant rustling of animals in the woods replacing the sounds of chaos back at the fort. Hugh began to wonder if the slight tremble in his limbs was still from exhaustion or from the October air that seemed to cut right through his wet clothes down to the bone. He pressed in a little closer to John trying to seek any warmth he could, but hanging on his back as he was, it didn't seem to help much.

They had traveled a little longer in silence before John stopped, holding perfectly still. Sensing the soldier's tension, Hugh kept quiet but couldn't help a curious look. Then he heard it. Voices. The sound of talking and crunching leaves and branches were coming, not from behind, but somewhere up ahead.

John crouched down, releasing Hugh's legs to let him stand on his own.

"Wait here," John whispered before straightening and slowly creeping forward.

Hugh could feel his heart pounding in his chest, unable to do anything more than stand in place. He watched, tense, as John crouched a little behind some of the underbrush trying to pinpoint the sound and see who else was here.

He made it up a few feet away from Hugh when his shoulders visibly relaxed, and he straightened turning back to Hugh. He smiled and gestured for Hugh to follow along.

"Martin, Tom!" John called out as he stepped forward with Hugh not far behind.

"John! Don't sneak up on us like that!"

"Johnny boy, made it across I see."

He was greeted with a number of other voices, and as Hugh came up beside the older boy, they entered a clearing with five other men. They were vaguely familiar to Hugh though he couldn't recall all their names. Martin and Tom, though, he knew were both part of John's mess. Most of them were dripping with water as well, though some looked like they might have been in boats and only had to step into the shallows.

"And you found young Hugh as well," Martin said, turning to the small boy. "And soaked to the bone, the both of you."

"I swam across the river," Hugh supplied.

"Brave lad," one of the other soldiers remarked with a nod. Hugh didn't miss the impressed note in his voice and found himself standing up a little straighter with a small smile in spite of his exhaustion.

"Not an easy job," another added. He, too, was dripping wet, his hair having come loose from its queue and whatever hat he might have had long gone, leaving strands of hair to stick to his weathered face. "But better than sticking around the fort."

The others all nodded, their expressions somber.

"Won't do to stay here, too long either" Martin said. "Lobsterbacks'll have control of this whole part of the Hudson now. Probably won't waste any time moving up river either."

"Officers'll probably be expecting us at Fort Constitution, closest one that isn't guaranteed to have been taken too," the weathered-looking soldier said. "If we don't take too long a rest, we could make it to there by evening."

Hugh slumped down to sit in the grassy clearing, deciding to try to get as much of his strength back as he could if there was going to be more walking. "Did any of you see my Papa when you got away? Dr. Morrison?" he asked.

The men glanced amongst each other. "I think I saw the doctor as I was getting just outside the fort," a soldier who looked about John's age spoke up. "Wasn't too far behind but everything was such a mad dash…didn't see where he went," he added with an apologetic look.

"You might as well join us to Fort Constitution," he said with a nod. "He'll likely be doing the same as us and sure they wouldn't say no to an extra surgeon once however many of us got away start arriving. If he didn't go that way, someone at the fort'll work on getting you home safe."

"You think so?" Hugh asked, perking up a little at the bit of hope the soldier offered.

"Seems the most logical place for him to go," the soldier replied, though some of the men beside him cast a few uncertain glances between each other.

Part of Hugh knew there was no guarantee of Papa being there, but as long as he did escape the fort, going there would be the best chance of catching up with each other or at least finding someone who might have seen him. And if he didn't escape... Hugh did not really want to think on that.

The group remained in the clearing a few minutes more, recovering their strength and trying to wring out their clothes. The soldiers discussed making a fire but decided against it. Even if the British probably would not be crossing the river right away, it seemed best not to give themselves away. Not to mention they could only spare so much time anyway. Hugh settled himself amongst the roots of a tree, leaning against the trunk. His eyelids felt heavy and soon were drifting closed as the soldiers talked about what this loss might mean and what they should do. He tried to listen, knowing it was important, but it was hard to concentrate, and soon their voices seemed to be lulling him to sleep rather than making any real sense.

He wasn't sure how much time passed before John was waking him up, the older boy crouched by his side and gently shaking his shoulder.

"Time to go," he said once Hugh stirred.

Reluctantly, Hugh got to his feet as the other men shrugged into the coats and shoes they had tried to dry out, and soon the group was on their way.

The walk was cold and seemed almost endless as they trudged along woodland paths and dirt roads, occasionally passing the edges of pastures and orchards of local farms. Once they had traveled north a while, they edged back closer to the river to help them keep their bearings. Hugh did his best to keep up on his own; surely the men were just as tired as he was and the nap had helped a little bit. Still, every so often, one of the older boys would offer a ride, usually when Hugh's pace began to slow, leaving him to trail behind.

The sun was low in the sky, and Hugh had offered to walk on his own, knowing the men must be getting tired after such a long march. So he was trailing along with them when large walls came into view up ahead. It had to be Fort Constitution—at least, he hoped it was. The men had said they thought they could make it there before the day's end, and Hugh didn't think they could go much longer before darkness fell. And he really hoped they would be done with walking soon.

"Is that where we're going?" he asked hopefully.

John turned back toward him with a smile. "Yeah, that's Fort Constitution, up there. Come on, sooner we get there, sooner can get some proper food and rest."

Hugh tried his best to pick up his pace; he was eager for the end of this long march of theirs. But it seemed he had already used his second wind up and couldn't really bring himself to anything more than a slightly quicker shuffle of his feet. Still, they were soon arriving at the gate of the fort, and Hugh saw the men talking with the soldiers guarding it. He hung back, more interested in catching his breath than listening to the men describing all the bad things that happened back at Fort Montgomery and whatever else they had to discuss. So he plopped down into the grass just a little behind, able to hear the murmur of their voices but not really paying attention.

Finally, the gates were opened, and Hugh pushed himself up to his feet, trailing after the group. The fort did not seem that much different from Fort Montgomery, cannons set along the sides and overlooking the river. They all worked so hard to try and keep control of the Hudson out of British hands, but now it seemed certain they would take it. Would they attack here next? How long before they did? Hugh supposed those very same questions were running through the minds of the other soldiers as they hurried off to deliver the news.

Hugh came to a stop, hanging back just a little as the soldiers from both forts all clustered together talking quickly. After a few moments, one of the Fort Constitution men gestured for them to follow him; Hugh heard him say something about talking to the officers. Hugh shuffled his feet a little, wondering if he should follow too. He wouldn't have anything to add to the information, but the Fort Montgomery soldiers were the only people he knew here. John seemed to take notice turning toward Hugh and opening his mouth to speak only for another voice to speak up.

"Heavens, child! Aren't you a sight!" a high-pitched voice gasped as a woman with a slightly stained apron over a woolen bodice and quilted petticoat came rushing over to him. "Surely you're not old enough to be soldiering, lad," she said, her tone firm as she came over to Hugh, looking him over.

"I…" It took Hugh a moment to gather himself, but he made sure to stand up straight and make his voice as confident and grown up as he could in spite of his tiredness. "I'm the surgeon's waiter," he declared.

"Is that so?" The woman's expression softened a little with a hint of a smile. "Quite the little man, you are then. But can't have a surgeon's waiter going about catching his death of cold and waterlogged bandages," she added, planting her hands on her hips in a way that reminded Hugh of his mother.

"He was separated from his father in the retreat," John said, lightly patting Hugh's shoulder. "We've been looking after him, but I think it's rest he needs most now."

The woman nodded. "We've got just the thing. Come on, young waiter…?"

"Hugh, ma'am. Hugh Morrison," he supplied, his spirits lifting at the idea of resting. And maybe some food.

"Well, right this way, Waiter Morrison," the woman replied. "I'm Mrs. Davis."

Soon, Hugh was being ushered over to where other women and a few young children were gathered. Hugh ignored the stares and plopped down as close to the stone circle around the fire as he could, eager for the warm, dry air it offered. The October chill had set deep in his bones, and he noticed the shimmer of frost on the outside of some of his clothes.

He sat for a few moments, aware of Mrs. Davis talking with some of the other camp followers. It seemed news of their arrival and what happened to Forts Montgomery and Clinton was spreading fast. One of the women ladled out some stew into a bowl and passed it to Hugh. He eagerly accepted, feeling the heat of the broth seeping through the bowl to warm his fingers, and quickly brought it to his lips, too hungry to even question what vegetables or meat was inside.

Once he began to feel the chill fade from his body and his shoulders could relax a little though, Hugh's other concerns began to come to mind.

"Are…are we the only ones from Fort Montgomery to come here?" he asked, glancing up over the flames at the gathered people.

"I've not heard of any other arrivals," a girl who looked only a little older than John said, glancing over at the others. They too shook their heads.

"Oh." Hugh's shoulder's drooped as he glanced down at the ground. He picked at the grass in front of him a little, not wanting to look up at all the eyes turned toward him. "I…I just was hoping my Papa…" he murmured.

The women cast somber glances at one another before Mrs. Davis spoke up. "It's early yet, and I'm sure most of the men that arrived would have headed for the officer's headquarters before coming to us. So it's possible word just hasn't spread just yet," she said. "For now though, I expect your father would want to make sure that wet bandage was changed and you get rested up after your long journey."

Hugh reached up to touch the bandages wrapped around his head. He could feel a few of the sections had slipped out of place—the outermost layers of the wrapping now coming nearly to his eyebrows—and the fabric shifted at even his light touch instead of sitting securely in place like when Papa first wrapped it. It seemed, despite Papa's skill, the swim across the river and long trek to Fort Constitution had proved too much. Still, Hugh frowned reaching up to touch the edges of the fabric and glancing aside. He had a feeling that removing the cloth and re-tending to it was going to hurt. As it was, his head already was starting to ache again. Besides, Papa had done these bandages; Papa was always the one who took care of his injuries, Hugh didn't want someone else poking at it now.

Mrs. Davis must have noticed his look. "It won't do any good leaving it soaked and coming loose," she chided. "Come along, we'll have our surgeon take a look."

Hugh still didn't much like the idea, but he knew Papa always talked about making sure wounds were cared for properly. So he probably would want Hugh to have the bandaging fixed as soon as he could, even if it wasn't Papa doing it. He begrudgingly rose to his feet, setting the now-empty bowl down and following the woman. She led him to their fort's surgeon to have him rewrap the wound.

"And you kept at your work even after that?" Mrs. Davis asked as the two of them stepped out of the building. While the surgeon had looked over his wound and put on fresh bandages, Mrs. Davis had asked Hugh about the battle and how he had been injured. Now, even as the bandaging was finished, he continued the story.

"Well, my head did hurt, and it was scary," he admitted. "But I knew we would be needing lint and bandages," he added.

"You're quite the brave lad to have pushed through for your duty. And then crossing the river after all that."

Hugh stood up just a little straighter at her praise. "We all have to do our part for the war," he replied.

Just then a voice broke through the quiet of the fort, distant but loud and drawing near. "Hugh! Hugh!"

The boy whirled around at the sound of the voice. It was Papa's voice! "Papa!" Hugh shouted back. And there was his Papa! He was running up the hilly ground so fast he was practically stumbling. There were more dark smudges on his clothes and skin than when Hugh last saw him along with tears in the fabrics. Almost before Hugh could fully realize that his Papa was really here, he felt himself swept up into his father's arms, pulled in close against his chest and breathing in the scent of smoke.

"Hugh, thank the Lord you're all right. You are all right, aren't you?" Papa's words came out in a rush, pulling back slightly from the embrace. His trembling hands rested on Hugh's shoulders as he looked him up and down. "They said you went down to the river. That swim...how did you...? I was afraid I'd lost you until the guard said a boy arrived here." His hand rose to touch Hugh's cheeks and moving to the freshly redone bandages clearly studying Hugh with a surgeon's eyes.

"I'm sorry, Papa," Hugh replied. "I didn't know where you were. Everyone was running and you were there and then you weren't and the soldiers...they were..."

"I know, I know, lad," Papa said soothingly. "You did right to keep going. Were you hurt at all? How's that head wound holding up?"

Hugh shook his head. "Tired, but I think I'm all right. Mrs. Davis and the surgeon got new bandages on," he said, his hand going up to touch the linen strips.

Papa gently took Hugh's hand guiding it away from the bandaging before standing and looking over at Mrs. Davis. "Thank you for looking after him. I'm in your debt."

"It was no trouble," she replied. "It was the other soldiers that got him here. They went to talk to the officers about what happened."

Papa nodded. "I'd best see about catching up with them as well," he said, before taking Hugh's hand and making his way further into the fort.

* * *

Hugh couldn't bring himself to pay much attention to the talk of what might come from the British taking Fort Montgomery. He could tell all the grownups were worried by the news and the Fort Constitution men were trying to decide what they should do. Hugh was worried too. He knew this was a bad turn for the cause, especially if the redcoats managed to come further up the Hudson. But after such a long day, Hugh couldn't bring himself to follow what exactly they were saying. About the only thing he did catch was the news that they would be staying the night at the fort. And that was welcome news; he was ready to be off his feet as soon as possible. So when he and Papa were given a cot, Hugh was asleep almost as soon as he laid down, snuggling in Papa's arms.

The next morning, Hugh and Papa set out further north toward home. Hugh was most definitely through with long journeys, but they fortunately managed to avoid any trouble. Papa was quiet most of the way, but Hugh figured he was just as tired and worried about what would happen as he was. They stopped occasionally to get some food and rest, but by nightfall they could see the familiar house up ahead. The glow of a hearth fire shone out from the kitchen window, which meant Mama must still be awake. They were just making their way up the walk when the door flew open and Mama rushed out.

"Robert! Hugh!" she cried out, rushing forward and pulling Hugh into her arms. "Oh, thank heavens you're both all right. I've heard all sorts of things about the British moving up the Hudson."

With one hand still on Hugh's shoulder she rose to kiss Papa. "I'd feared the worst and—oh, Hugh! Your head!" She broke off, turning back to notice the bandages around Hugh's head. "What happened? Oh, but you must be freezing out here. Come inside, come along," she added, ushering them back to the house.

Inside, squares of pumpkin and apple slices hung along strings over the fireplace to dry. A few large, covered jars sat out on the table giving off the sharp scent of vinegar, suggesting Mama had been working on pickling as well, preserving food as much as she could to last the coming winter.

"Sit yourself down, you both look a fright," Mama fussed as she ushered Hugh over to a stool near the hearth and Papa sat down in his chair near the table. "What on earth happened?"

"The fort was attacked yesterday," Papa sighed, his posture more slouched than Hugh had ever seen. "The British've taken it."

"No…" Mama gasped, her hand coming to her moth as she turned to face him with wide-eyed shock.

Papa nodded. "The soldiers held as long as they could, but they couldn't hold out against it all. British and Hessians, even Loyalists." Papa shook his head with a sigh.

"What does this mean?" Mama asked. "Will they be at our doors now?"

"I don't know," Papa admitted. "We can hope the other troops will be able to stop them, maybe even push them back, if luck is on our side. I have permission to take a day or so before I find out where I'll be needed now."

"You don't mean to go back to the army so soon? Just look at the state of you two!" Mama frowned, keen eyes scanning over Papa's disheveled appearance and coming to rest on Hugh's bandages.

"I do," Papa replied with a nod. "I promised to do what I could for the cause, which means being where they need surgeons on hand. I'll head out just as soon as I can get some supplies here."

"You mean we'll go?" Hugh looked up at Papa in surprise. "Aren't I coming?"

"You certainly are not," Mama replied, her hands planting firmly on her hips as she turned to Hugh. "A wound on your head like that, you'll be resting and staying put right here."

"But Papa said we've all got to do our part," Hugh replied, fidgeting on the stool. He was not exactly eager to see another battle, but he didn't want Papa going alone, either. And hadn't he proven he could handle himself? He got away from the fort and across the Hudson on his own. Or had that been the wrong thing to do? "Don't you still need a waiter?"

"I'll be hard-pressed to find as good a waiter," Papa replied with a small smile. "But your mother's right. You need rest with that head wound, and after pushing yourself so hard. I made a promise that I would heal the men of the Continental Army, and that is how I'll do my part. But now, you have to do your part here."

"I could use an extra pair of hands getting in the harvest and preserving enough food for winter," Mama added.

Hugh glanced between them both thinking over their words. "I don't want to desert the cause, though," he said quietly. He'd heard soldiers talk about deserters leaving their duties—it always sounded like a bad thing.

"You won't be," Papa assured him. "With both Fort Montgomery and Clinton taken, things in the Hudson Valley will get even more tense. We've got to make sure there's a home to come back to, after all."

Hugh supposed that made sense. The preserves all around the kitchen was a reminder of all the work that autumn brought with it, and remembering what Papa said about more supplies having to go to the army, they would need to bring in as much as they could from their small vegetable garden and orchard. He gave a small nod.

"But for now it's rest we all need," Mama said. "There's a fresh shirt in the trunk by your bed. Go get out of those dirty clothes and off to bed. I'll see if there's any salvaging them in the morning."

Hugh obeyed, as Mama and Papa continued to talk—Papa giving her some more details from the past few days. Soon enough, Hugh had changed into the new shirt and crawled into his bed. The comfort of soft woolen sheets quickly lulling him to sleep.

As he said, Papa was soon off, back to offer his services to the army—with surprisingly better news than any had been expecting. The very day they had returned home the British had been beaten in battle. The defeat sent them retreating back down the river, surrendering all the ground they had gained by taking the forts.

Reflections

Mirror, Mirror, on the wall
Tell me who has walked this hall.

I've seen giggling siblings with gossip to share
Been fogged by the steam of meals upon fine chinaware
When young lovers stole a kiss at the door I saw a maiden walking
on air
Through that parlor door an old man dozed in his armchair
Countless collars fixed and curls laid just so until there came quiet
and disrepair

Careful hands cleared the tarnish and my vision comes clearer
Now schoolchildren gather before me at a tour guide's call
Visitors young and old gather in a queue
And I listen to the stories told of all the faces I once knew

Mirror, Mirror, with handle long and lean,
Tell me the faces you have seen

Shoppers raised me up with smiles fair
But only one chose me, her face young and full of flair
Shown off with pride, my beauty friends and kin did declare
How pleased I was to lend my aid as she fashioned her hair
Years went by and I watched her face age with tender care

I pray you hold me nearer
For free of the dust you did clean
I see her face anew
I see her eyes again, in you

Mirror, Mirror,
Who has remembered all
Now hold me, too, in your view

Image and Identity

Grace's fingers smoothly moved over the piano keys as she played the last few measures of the song she had chosen to practice with today. It was a new song for her and somewhat complicated, but she had played through it a few of times already, and she was a quick learner. As she finished the song, she sat quietly, letting the final notes fade away, and once complete silence had settled over the parlor, she gave a small smile, satisfied with the progress she had made for the time being. Her mother had been talking about the Faulkners' Christmas party and how nobles from Europe would surely be invited now that their daughter was married to a British lord and was going to spend Christmas in New York this year. And all of her talk had made it clear that Grace was expected to make a very good impression on all the other guests. She was just putting the music book away on the shelf beside the piano when she heard the parlor door open. Grace turned to see Edwin enter the room, his overcoat was draped over his arm and only a few reddish blonde locks stuck out from beneath his hat.

"I noticed the music stop, and I was planning to go skating," he said. "The carriage is almost ready if you would like to come."

Grace beamed as she quickly crossed the room to join her brother in the hall. "Of course I would like to!" she said excitedly before remembering her mother's frequent reminders of how a genteel woman ought to always be calm and composed. "I'll meet you downstairs as soon as I'm ready," she said more calmly.

"I'll let Mother know," Edwin replied. Grace nodded, knowing skating was one of the few outdoor activities her mother had no objections to her practicing.

* * *

Grace glided over the ice beside Edwin as they wove around the handful of other people who had remained to skate despite the sink-

42

ing sun. They would still have enough light to skate by for a while yet, and it was easier with less people. She loved seeing Central Park in winter—everything blanketed in white and people laughing and chatting as they skated, went sledding, and played in the snow. The cold did not bother her as she had chosen to wear her fitted black velvet jacket that kept her warm and even matched her tartan skirt nicely.

"Edwin! Grace!"

They turned and stopped at the sound of a familiar voice. A tall girl in a deep green dress and ruffled coat was skating away from a group of other girls.

"Good evening, Lucile," Grace greeted the older girl as she came to a stop in front of them.

"It's good to see you," Edwin added.

"And you as well," she answered. "It's such a lovely day, and I haven't been skating since last winter. How are you two?"

"Quite well," Edwin replied. "And yourself?"

"Splendid," Lucille answered with a wide smile. "And how is Edi—um, I mean, ah, your family?" Lucille's right arm unconsciously reached to clasp at the elbow of her left sleeve as she glanced aside hastily rephrasing her question. It was no surprise that she would think of their sister Edith. Being the same age as Edith and Edwin, the two girls had been classmates and even attended most of the same parties. She also would no doubt know all about Edith eloping with the superintendent of a newsboys lodging house against their parents' wishes. While Grace thought the whole thing was quite romantic and Edwin was content with anything that made his twin happy, their parents had been furious and did their best to avoid the subject altogether.

"All are well. Nothing new to mention, really," Edwin answered.

Grace caught the brief look of sympathy that crossed Lucille's expression, clearly having understood Edwin's last comment to mean their parents had still not forgiven Edith. "I trust you will be at the Faulkners' party in a few weeks?" Lucile asked. "It's sure to be great fun," she added after a moment.

"Yes," Grace answered, grateful for the change of subject. "Mother and I even went shopping for new gowns yesterday."

"I still need to find something to wear for it," Lucile said cheerfully. "Everyone's sure to be in their finest."

Grace nodded in agreement. "I'm a bit tired," she said after a moment. "I think I'll sit for a minute."

The two nodded, and with a small wave Grace glided over to an empty bench near the shore. She was not actually all that tired, but she knew Edwin was very fond of Lucile and that the two would enjoy some time to talk privately. She sat for a few minutes watching the skaters; some were quite experienced while others, especially young children, struggled just to keep their balance. It was interesting to see all the different skill levels and styles of skating and listen to the happy chatter of the people enjoying an afternoon in the park. She was startled out of her observations by a snowball hitting her shoulder. With a gasp Grace jumped and turned to see a group of children having a snowball fight a short distance from where she was sitting. Most continued building up forts and throwing snowballs at each other, not even noticing that one had gone astray. She was about to return her attention to the ice when a boy's voice called over the shouts of the other children.

"Watch your aim, Nellie!" The laughter was clear in the boy's voice despite the admonishing words. Grace turned to see the speaker, a boy near her age in a loose-fitting coat and faded cap. He was addressing a little girl who Grace guessed was the one who threw the snowball that hit her.

"Ain't no sport hitting folks that don't know how to have a good snowball fight."

"Whoever said I don't?" Grace replied swiftly rising to her feet, scooping up a handful of snow from the end of the bench and tossing it at the boy who had spoken. It struck his chest lightly, since he had been too surprised by her response to move. He blinked at her for a moment before a grin spread across his face. He bent to make another snowball, and seeing it coming, Grace was able to duck and avoid it. She moved to join the other children, but as soon as she took a step she wobbled on the blades of her ice skates. She quickly bent to remove the blades from the bottom of her shoes so she could run about normally, only to feel the stiffness of her corset keeping her back straight. Stopped by the tight bindings before she could even reach her shoes, all her mother's reminders of how she was not a child anymore and had to show more propriety came to mind. Grace could practically hear what her mother would say if she were here: "Romping about in the snow is not the behavior of a proper young lady." Slowly returning to a standing position, she realized a few of the other children had now stopped their game and were staring at her with the same look of amused surprise the boy had worn.

Straightening her posture, she faced the first boy. "Just because I can have a snowball fight does not mean I wish to," she said keeping her voice even. "Now, if you'll excuse me I think I will return to skating." Not waiting for a response she turned and made her way back to the ice. Yes, skating was a much more acceptable pastime for a young lady, and Grace really did enjoy ice skating, even if she would have enjoyed a snowball fight as well. As her parents often reminded her, she had to consider propriety over her own whims. A grunt of surprise and burst of laughter behind her suggested the children had returned to their fun. Grace spotted Edwin and Lucile and was grateful to see they had moved toward the other side of the pond, and she quickly glided over to them, letting the laughter of the snowball fight merge with the voices of skaters and others enjoying the park.

They both smiled as they saw her approach. The three of them continued to skate and talk for another hour before the dimming sunlight reminded them that they would be expected home soon. So they said their farewells and made their way from the park.

"Seeing Lucile reminded me," Edwin said as they walked away from the pond, "I still don't know what to give her as a Christmas present. You would probably know better what she might like. Would you mind helping me look for something tomorrow?"

Grace smiled at her brother; he never had been very good at shopping, so she was not really surprised by the request. She nodded her consent; already trying to think of what sort of things would make the perfect gift for Edwin to offer Lucile.

* * *

They had set out early in the morning to begin looking for a gift and had been surprised to almost immediately find a bracelet with a delicate floral design that they both agreed would suit Lucile perfectly. They had looked around the store a little while longer but still both Grace and Edwin agreed the bracelet was the best choice.

"We're not far from Edith's home," Grace spoke as they stepped outside the store, "and I doubt anyone will be expecting us home so soon." Grace knew her parents were still angry, but they had not expressly forbidden her or Edwin from visiting their sister, even if they made it clear they had no intentions of speaking with their eldest daughter any time soon.

"Good idea," Edwin replied. "It's been too long since we saw her last." So with that, they turned along the sidewalk in the direction of the lodging house. The walk would take a few minutes, but even when snowflakes began to slowly fall around them, the siblings decided it would be worth the walk to see their sister.

The lodging house was a plain structure but well-kept, and it was a welcome sight to Grace as she had started to feel the winter air nipping at her nose a little before the building came into sight. Edwin was just reaching for the door when it suddenly swung open to reveal a young woman wearing a simple dark blue dress, her strawberry blonde hair pulled up into a bun at the top of her head. She looked different without the fine fashionable gowns and elaborate hairstyles Grace had grown up seeing her sister wear, but her bright smile had not changed a bit.

"I saw you from the window," she spoke excitedly. "It's wonderful to see you both."

"We finished our errand a bit early," Grace spoke as Edith embraced her in greeting. "So we thought we would come and visit you."

"I hope we're not intruding," Edwin added as his twin wrapped him in a hug as well. "But we did want to see how you were doing."

"Not at all," Edith assured him, "Henry is out on business, but I don't have anything pressing at the moment."

"Good mornin', Mrs. Adler."

The three of them turned at the voice, and Grace's eyes widened slightly as she saw the same boy from yesterday walking toward them with a stack of newspapers under his arm. It was easy enough to recognize him since he was wearing the exact same coat, hat, and trousers as the day before. As he neared them, he seemed to notice Grace, staring thoughtfully at her for a moment before speaking. "Weren't you in the park yesterday?"

Grace nodded, a little surprised at the chances of meeting the same stranger two days in a row.

"You two have met?" Edith asked in amusement. "Small world isn't it?" Grace gave her a questioning look at that comment.

"Thomas stays here at the lodging house," Edith explained. "Thomas, this is my brother and sister, Edwin and Grace Dunn," she added, turning to Thomas and gesturing to each of her siblings in turn.

"You're her family?" Thomas said slowly, glancing between the three of them. Grace forced her expression to remain neutral; it was easy to guess his thoughts. Of course he knew about the marriage if he lived in the lodging house, not to mention it had been mentioned in numerous papers, with articles not just reporting on the elopement but describing how furious Mr. and Mrs. Dunn were about their daughter marrying against their wishes. The boy had probably spent the better part of the days after the elopement with a stack of papers, calling out the headlines and tidbits of various stories to passersby.

"Oh, I'm sorry, Thomas. I hadn't meant to delay you," Edith spoke up, sounding as if she was struck by a sudden thought. "Was there something you needed? You boys usually go straight to your places once you've gotten the morning paper."

"Oh, right!" Thomas replied, digging his free hand into the pocket of his coat and pulled out a small brown bag. "I ran into Mr.

Pagano, and he asked me to give this to you. For helpin' get that medicine for his boy. Had to give it to you now, else I's gonna eat 'em myself," he added with a cheeky grin.

"I'll be sure to thank him when next I see him," Edith replied, reaching into the bag and taking out a handful of chestnuts. "And as thanks for bringing them," she added, holding them out to Thomas, "you deserve a treat."

"Thanks, Mrs. Adler," Thomas replied with a grateful smile as he took the chestnuts. "I'd better be gettin' to my spot, the good crowds'll be there soon." And with that, he hurried along the sidewalk to wherever it was he sold his papers.

"Goodness, it's cold," Edith said, shivering in only her house dress as a gust of wind rushed by them. "Come inside. I'm quite proud of how I've managed our apartment. Nothing grand like our house, of course, but it really feels like a home if I say so myself."

She gestured for them to come in. They followed her inside to see the superintendent's apartment, both eager to see what their sister's new home looked like now that she had had some time to settle in.

As Edith had said, it was nothing like the Dunn family house. There were a few photographs scattered around the room, most of which Grace recognized as pictures that had been in Edith's bedroom as well as a few of her husband, Henry's, relatives. At least, Grace assumed they were his relatives, posing in the pictures with him. The wood furniture was all simply designed, though there was a pair of colorful patchwork pillows decorating the small sofa that Grace recognized as her sister's taste. On the other side of the room, there was a writing desk with neatly stacked papers, notebooks, and envelopes arranged on it. Grace and Edwin followed Edith as she crossed the room toward the sofa and a pair of wooden chairs around a table. The twins settled themselves on the sofa, and Grace took one of the chairs. She noticed a book set on the little side table beside the sofa. Tilting her head to see the cover more clearly, she found the neatly printed title, *Philanthropy and Social Progress.*

"I've only read the first few essays so far," Edith spoke up, noticing Grace looking at the book. "But it has already gotten me thinking about ways to help the boys here. It's time to bring democracy to all parts of society, so we're making sure the boys get a good education and are treated with basic kindness so they can have every opportunity to advance themselves."

"So, you're not simply giving them a job with the newspapers?" Edwin asked, with a smile that suggested he already had some idea of the answer. No doubt he recognized Edith's tone as well as Grace did. Her green eyes were wide and shining with enthusiasm, and her voice rose with excitement.

"Well, a job is important of course," Edith replied, "and selling newspapers is a fine start. They learn a work ethic and have an income to live on. But they can't be trapped here forever, not when, with just a little help and guidance, they could be writing for or even owning a paper or contributing to some other business entirely or perhaps even teaching other children. If we're to succeed as a democracy, we must remember Christian kindness and be certain that everyone enjoys basic comforts. Oh, if you heard what sort of conditions these boys are coming from, those things have been completely denied them. Henry had already been keeping up a fund to help the boys go west. There's good fresh air and food and plenty of work to be done there. But we're always looking for more ways to help them."

Just then they heard the apartment door creak open, revealing a tall man wearing a plain but well-kept suit.

"Henry!" Edith beamed rising up to meet her husband.

"Hello, dear," he replied and gave her cheek a kiss. "Edwin, Grace," he said with a smile as he noticed them both standing. "It's good to see you, both."

"And you, too," Edwin replied, shaking Henry's hand in greeting.

"The invitations are all arranged," Henry said, turning to Edith. "They should all be printed with plenty of time."

"That's good," Edith replied before turning to Grace and Edwin. "We're printing out proper invitations to all the newsboys for the Christmas dinner. I know it's a bit silly to bother when we could just announce it here, but why shouldn't their Christmas party have all the bells and whistles as anyone else's? Besides, you remember how much we loved seeing pretty invitations arrive in the mail. They'll just be handed to the boys, as they don't always have a permanent address, but I think it will still make for a nice gesture."

Grace nodded in agreement, all three siblings had always enjoyed seeing the beautifully printed invitation cards, and it had been especially exciting when their names were included.

"It sounds like a fine idea," Edwin replied. "So are you taking charge of organizing the newsboys Christmas dinner?"

"Well, Henry and the rest of the staff have been organizing it before now," Edith replied, "so they have most parts of the event all planned from past years, but I'm determined to help as much as I can. I will be helping decorate and any other preparations necessary; I shall even be serving the boys their food."

"That reminds me," Henry said suddenly. "I've got to review the budget for the party before too much planning is done." He moved toward the writing desk, reaching for a notebook before even sitting down.

"We won't disturb you," Edwin said. "I'm glad we were able to see you both, but we had best start heading home."

With a parting embrace for each of them, the siblings said their farewells, and Edith saw them out to the street.

Edwin and Grace made their way through the crowds of people, weaving around shoppers laden with bags, small children peering in at store windows, and a handful of businessmen apparently on some errand or another.

"So, how was it you met that boy?" Edwin asked after a short time as he seemed to recall their encounter at the lodging house. "Thomas, I think Edith said his name was."

"He was in the park yesterday," Grace explained. "He and a few others were playing in the snow when I went to take a rest. We spoke briefly when a stray snowball hit me, but I hadn't even known his name or even that he was a newsboy before today."

"Still," Edwin replied with an amused smile, "rather funny running into him twice, in a city with so many people. As Edith said, it's a small world."

Grace nodded in agreement, it was quite surprising but it did not seem all that important. She was surprised by the situation herself, but she supposed sometimes the world just worked that way and she could just accept it.

* * *

Grace sat beside her mother on the horsehair sofa of the Travers' parlor. Her mother had recently added Grace's name to her calling cards, saying that it was time Grace begin preparing to enter society so she would have to accompany her mother when returning visits and leaving cards. Mr. Travers had recently come to work at the same bank as Grace's father, so it was important to be on good terms with his wife. The two women had finished discussing different fashions when Mrs. Travers turned to Grace.

"Perhaps you'll be looking forward to some pretty new dresses for Christmas?" she asked cheerfully.

"That would be very nice," Grace replied politely. She did like dresses, but she already had so many of them, honestly, she thought she would rather sweets or trinkets as a gift. Still, she knew they would be a very likely gift, and her mother would not approve of her talking about childish things while calling. After all, the whole point of joining her mother was to show that she was becoming a young lady and ready to enter adult society.

"How old are you, again, dear?" Mrs. Travers asked.

"I shall be fourteen next month," Grace replied.

"Ah," Mrs. Travers replied cheerfully. "A bit old to be writing to Santa Clause then, I suppose. I rarely see a letter in the newspaper from children older than ten. Still, I do so enjoy seeing those lovely notes in all the papers. Some of the dear creatures are so charming, too. Asking for dolls, or wagons, or other toys for themselves but then adding that Santa remember the orphans as well."

"Yes, children are so kindhearted," Mrs. Dunn replied. "Grace used to always ask for fruits or baubles for suffering children when she wrote such letters."

51

Grace just smiled, though she did not really think she deserved the credit for that idea. It was what Edith always did, before Grace had learned to write well and so had relied on Edith to include Grace's requests in her own letters. Grace did really want to think that poor and suffering children would receive nice gifts, so she continued to include that request even when she could write for herself, but she doubted it would have occurred to her if Edith had not introduced the subject first. Of course, Grace knew her mother had no intention of discussing anything about Edith while making social calls.

They continued to chat about holiday plans for a few more minutes before Mrs. Dunn decided they should be on their way. Mrs. Travers was the last visit they had planned for the day, so all that was left to do was leave their own calling cards for a few prominent ladies in the city and then shopping for Grace's youngest cousin, Helen.

After bidding Mrs. Travers good-bye, they moved on to Schwarz's Toy Bazaar. Grace walked beside her mother, letting her gaze wander over the displays of all the newest toys amid all sorts of Christmas decorations. She noticed a wax doll with a sweet little smile and an elegant dress. It's golden hair and deep blue eyes even matched Helen's features.

"Mother," she said, pointing toward the doll, "do you think Helen would like that one?" Her mother turned to examine the doll, as well as the price tag attached to it.

"Yes, I expect she would like it very much," Mrs. Dunn agreed after a moment and turned to go seek out one of the saleswomen to ask for the doll to be packaged for them.

"Such patience," an unfamiliar woman's voice softly cooed. Grace turned to see a woman in a layered silk dress with lace trimming the collar and sleeves standing beside a man in a fine suit and top hat. Both of their backs were to Grace, so she peered around them, curious about what had captured their attention. A cluster of thin children in old and patched clothing stood around an elaborate dollhouse display, complete with little inhabitants in fine clothing and ornate furniture. A small girl, who looked no older than five years old, had her hand reaching halfway toward the painted trim along the dollhouse's roof but pulled it back and clasped her hands behind her back. A boy, just a few years older and with enough resemblance to be the girl's brother, had his hand resting on the little one's shoulder, apparently having stopped her from touching the house.

Grace had seen such children many times before while shopping here, both for friends or family and for her own playthings. They never touched a single toy, though they sometimes crowded around the same display for hours. She had never really paid them much mind before, but somehow it caught her attention to see the two adults looking on as the children admired the toys they could never have.

"Quite admirable, indeed," the man agreed with his companion with a nod before the couple continued on their way.

Just then Grace's mother returned with a saleswoman who took up the wax doll and led them over to the counter. While they waited for the doll to be packaged, Grace glanced at the little crowd of children as they whispered about how wonderful the house was. Grace glanced to the other side of the space and noticed a little boy dressed in clothes as worn and stained as the children's around the dollhouse. She had to suppress a gasp when the boy turned and she could see the right sleeve of his jacket hung empty at his side. He made his way over to a display of wooden blocks, the box containing them advertising that it offered blocks with both upper and lower case letters carved on them.

"Grace, darling," her mother's voice pulled her attention away from the boy. "Whatever is the matter?" she asked. Grace supposed her expression revealed her sympathy for the child. Edith had spoken a great deal about factory conditions and how dangerous they could be for children. The boy had probably been sent to work to help keep his family from starving and by some accident had been injured and prevented from earning a living by most kinds of labor ever again.

She scanned the faces of other onlookers, all of whom the boy managed to ignore, his wistful gaze locked on the blocks. But none of the others seemed inclined to do anything, they just watched, admiring the boy's restraint.

"Mother, I'm sure that block set doesn't cost much," she said quietly. "And perhaps playing with letters would be productive.

Wouldn't it be just like a charming Christmas story to buy it for the boy. Perhaps getting to play with letters would help prepare him for office work, some way he could earn a living later without needing both arms," she added, recalling her father once complaining about people who brought poverty upon themselves by not practicing thrift or honest hard work. Perhaps pointing out that the boy's future options were limited would encourage her mother to help.

"We donate to the Children's Aid Society, sweetheart," Mrs. Dunn said kindly. "I'm sure they see to it children like him are prepared for the future." She turned back to the counter when the saleswoman placed a neatly wrapped box before her. She took the doll box and turned toward the door.

"Come along, we've been out for a while now, I'm sure you're as hungry as I. The restaurant down the street is always delicious, why don't we stop in there before going home?"

Knowing her mother's tone to mean she had made up her mind on the matter, Grace complied and followed her mother out of the store, trying to forget about the poor children in the toy store.

* * *

Mrs. Dunn stood at the store counter, admiring a sapphire necklace the saleswoman had brought out to her. Shopping with her mother had been fun at first, getting to see more of the holiday displays and such. Only, they had run out of any particular purpose to shop for an hour or so ago, and now, just browsing was becoming a bit tedious.

"Mother," she said. "The post office is only a few doors down from here. I could drop the Christmas letters off while you think about the necklace." Delivering the letters was the only planned errand left for the day, but her mother would have no objection to continuing shopping even after the task was done. And at least, doing so would provide a break for Grace.

"All right, darling," Mrs. Dunn replied, reaching into her bag for the last of the Christmas letters she had written.

Grace left the shop and had dropped the letters off in the post office in just a few minutes. As she stepped outside the post office, she heard someone shouting. "Bill Dodger strikes again, right here in New York's own Waldorf." She turned toward the sound to see none other than Thomas, waving a newspaper above his head with a small stack under his other arm. He still wore the same clothes and was waving a copy of the latest paper in the air shouting the different headlines.

He did not seem to notice Grace until he had almost passed her. "Huh, quite the surprise seein' you again," he said, stopping in front of her.

"Ah, yes," Grace replied, not sure what to make of this encounter. "I suppose you're looking forward to the lodging house's Christmas dinner?" she asked, unable to think of anything else to say.

"'Course. Best meal we gets all year," he answered, "and some of my chums will be joining for the dinner that don't live in the lodging house. The organizers always invite all the newsboys even if theys already got a place."

"Will you join them after the dinner?" She asked. Grace knew Edith and Henry would try to give the boys an enjoyable Christmas, but they had to work with a budget so the dinner was the only gift they could give besides, perhaps, company. But she imagined it would be more enjoyable to be with people he was close with.

For a moment, the boy's smile slipped and a more somber look came to his eyes. "I couldn't just surprise 'em, and if they invited me, their folks'd feel like they gotta have somethin' for me."

Grace could guess where his thoughts went from there. If working-class families struggled to provide for their own children, like the ones in the toy store, it would be hard to add a guest. However, Thomas was quick to push aside the seriousness and his grin returned. "So I just spend my Christmas at the lodging house, enjoyin' the good full feeling of a big meal."

"I see," Grace said, regretting bringing up the subject and not wanting to press the matter. "My mother will be wondering what's kept me, but I just remembered, she had mentioned wanting a copy of today's paper." Her mother had said no such thing, but Grace had a little money in her coin purse, and she doubted her mother would object to the paper if she bought it.

"Well, then, miss," he replied holding one of the papers out to her with a flourish. "This is one of the finest papers in the city. All the latest news you could look for."

Grace smiled as she paid him for the paper and gave a small wave before hurrying on to the jewelry shop with the paper in hand. As expected, her mother was surprised to see Grace return from the post office with a newspaper, but she agreed when Grace pointed out they had not read the paper today and so it might have something interesting.

* * *

It was finally Christmas Eve, and the time of the Faulkners' party had arrived. Grace took Edwin's extended hand as she stepped out of the carriage, and the siblings fell into step behind their parents. There was a great throng of people gathered outside the grand hotel's front doors, all jostling about to see who would emerge from each of the carriages as they stopped in front of the hotel. Despite the number of people, the handful of other party guests arriving around the same time as the Dunns were easy to spot; their glittering jewels, elaborate gowns, and fine suits standing out against the worn and faded clothes and dust smeared faces of people staring at the procession of expensive carriages and elegant party clothes. As they made their way through the crowd, Grace saw some of the onlookers, who were too far back to see the approaching guests, clearly were turned toward the hotel, clustered around windows, apparently trying to see if they could spot the ballroom or any passing party attendants inside the building.

They quickly moved past the crowd and reached the hotel, showing their invitation they were led into the room the Faulkners had reserved for their party. The time spent getting ready had been well worth it as Grace looked around the room. Anyone who was anyone in New York was here and dressed to impress. The Dunns were no different; the maid had spent hours helping first Mrs. Dunn and then Grace get into their new gowns and arranging their hair to make sure every strand was set in a perfect curl that fell gracefully over her shoulders. Now Grace felt like a real grown-up lady in her dress—deep green silk with velvet trim and delicate lace accenting the fitted bodice. She had carefully selected the perfect jewelry to match—a jewel-studded bracelet—and Mother had even given Grace one of her diamond necklaces to wear. Some of the other girls dripped with even more jewels that made them practically glow in the lamplights, but Grace could still feel at ease among them as her own accessories glittered as she mingled and moved across the room.

Once they greeted the hosts and were introduced to some of the prominent guests, they made their way to the center of the hall, mingling with the familiar faces of all the wealthy families of New York City. Mrs. Dunn drifted toward the group of ladies speaking with the Faulkners' newly married daughter, no doubt eager to hear about how she was settling in to life in Europe. It only took Edwin a minute to see Lucile, and Grace could not help but smile as he made his way over to her, requesting a dance. Grace could not hear Lucile's answer over the chatter of the crowd, but the young woman's bright smile and enthusiastic nod seemed to indicate she was glad to have him ask and not just agreeing for the sake of being polite. Lucile then promptly took out her dance card and gave it to Edwin to sign for his turn to dance with her.

Grace spent most of the party with a few girls from her school, talking about what gifts they were expecting for Christmas or about books they were reading. She and her friends had not yet had their debuts so they did not need dance cards, but even so, a few boys of their own age had asked them to dance. It was rather fun and good to keep in practice with dancing as Grace soon would be formally presented to New York society and expected to socialize at events like this. The night felt almost magical to be surrounded by the smells of sweet perfume and music from the band on one side of the room filled the air. The hotel had been decorated as beautifully as all the guests with chandeliers strung with the clearest crystals and garlands of evergreens with rich velvet ribbons along the walls.

After a few dances, Grace moved off to the side of the room to take a short break, content to watch her friends twirl across the dance floor for a few minutes. She had just finished a glass of spiced apple cider, setting the glass down on the nearby table, when she noticed the Faulkners' newly married daughter, Margaret, gliding across the hall with a teenage boy who looked to be only a little older than Grace beside her. She offered a polite smile as the pair approached her.

"How are you enjoying the party, Grace?" Margaret asked.

"Oh, very much," Grace replied. "Everything is so lovely. Your parents must have found the finest musicians in New York. I almost hate to have needed a rest from dancing."

"Didn't I tell you she had quite the musical ear?" Margaret smiled, turning to the boy beside her. He wore a tailored suit with a pristine white handkerchief neatly folded in the pocket. "Grace, I wanted you to meet Charles Fitzsimmons. His father, Sir John Fitzsimmons, is a dear friend of my husband's who came to visit America as well. Charles, may I introduce Grace Dunn," she added.

"A pleasure to meet you, Miss Dunn," Charles replied with a bow of his head. "I understand we share an interest in music."

"The pleasure is mine," Grace replied with a curtsy as her mother had reminded her was proper for nobility in Europe, before placing her hand in his. "Yes, I am very fond of music, whether listening or playing."

"I had best see to some other guests. I will leave you two to chat," Margaret said before flitting off to another group of party guests.

Grace knew her mother had likely encouraged Margaret to make the introduction and would want her to make a good impression on the young noble so she did her best to make conversation. Mostly they discussed his impression of America; this visit to New York was his first time away from Europe. He seemed polite and friendly enough that Grace had no trouble thinking of things to talk about, which she was grateful for, but it was hardly anything memorable. Just his impression of the sites he had seen so far and suggestions she might have. After a while, he had invited her to a dance as a new song started up and they could continue talking. At the end of that dance, he offered a polite excuse to part ways; no doubt he had plenty of other guests he would be expected to meet.

"Perhaps I will see you tomorrow, Miss Dunn?" he asked just before they parted ways. "My father read about a Christmas dinner for the newsboys, the article says it is open to the public to view. Father is quite curious to see this tradition you have here in America."

"Oh, we…well we had not been planning on going, as far as I am aware," Grace answered. Of course, he was one of the few people at this party that was unaware of Edith's elopement, and she was not sure if she should mention it or not. "But perhaps we may be there."

He smiled and gave a polite nod before moving toward the other side of the hall. After Charles brought up the newsboys' dinner tomorrow, Grace found herself wishing Edith could be here at the party with them. She tried to distract herself from such thoughts by watching the dancers and other guests enjoying the yuletide festivities, but instead, that reminded her even more of Edith. Her sister never had any trouble socializing, and she did not need sparkling jewels to shine when she was on the dance floor.

During the meal, Grace remained absorbed in her thoughts and so took little part in the conversation. Edwin, of course, noticed his little sister's lack of enthusiasm for the festivities. "You're awfully quiet," he said. "Is everything all right?"

She nodded and forced a smile. Edwin did not look convinced, but it was just then that the servers came to remove the last of the dishes and so everyone rose from the table. Grace did her best to try to remain cheerful for the rest of the evening, but she was relieved when it was announced that the party would be coming to an end. It was Christmas Eve after all, so the children ought to be in bed. However, the prospect of waking tomorrow and going through Christmas day without her sister for the first time did her mood little good.

"Something has been bothering you." Edwin's voice broke into her thoughts as the carriage rolled along the street. The look he was giving Grace from the seat beside her made it clear it was not a question.

Grace could not help a tiny frown at him. Of course he did not know what exactly was on her mind, but she was still not happy that he had brought it up in front of their parents, who were now both looking at her in concern. However, it was Christmas, a time of goodwill when families were supposed to come together. "I'm just missing Edith," she replied, glancing at the floor of the carriage as she braced herself for her parents' reaction.

"Edith made her choice to leave," Mrs. Dunn said in the same patient but almost lecturing tone she used when explaining lessons or rules. "We wanted to see her take her proper place in society, but she chose otherwise. Here, she would have been provided for; your father and I were well on our way to securing a title for her, but she chose to make her life looking after the children of people who could not do so themselves. You mustn't let her poor judgment spoil your evening."

"Still, it would be nice to see her," Grace pressed on. "Tomorrow is Christmas, after all. What harm could it do to pay a quick visit?" She knew better than to expect her parents to reconcile with Edith immediately; their hopes for a noble title in the family had been too high for that. But perhaps just getting them on speaking terms would be a good start.

"Visit her?" her father replied skeptically. "Just imagine how it would look for a respectable family to be roaming about a newsboys' lodging house on Christmas day."

"Actually, quite a few respectable families will be in the area," Edwin joined in the conversation. "The papers reported that the dinner will be open to the public to see. I expect they want to show what good the lodging houses have done for the boys, what with taking them off the streets and giving them proper role models for how to be an asset to society."

"Yes," Grace added, lifting her gaze with an excited smile. The turn in the conversation giving her an idea that had her earlier irritation with Edwin vanishing. "Sir John and his son are even planning to attend."

Her parents glanced at each other at that news. They would not want to miss an opportunity to secure connections to the visiting nobles and so were clearly torn between socializing with the Fitzsimmonses and avoiding Edith. "Well, perhaps it would be suitable to attend, with the other families," Mr. Dunn spoke after a minute.

Mrs. Dunn nodded in agreement as Grace and Edwin struggled not to look too triumphant at the small progress they had made. "Of course, we won't be making any sort of scene to go and speak with Edith," Mrs. Dunn added. "With any luck, the talk about that fellow going about staying in hotels and leaving before the bill comes along will have made everyone forget the elopement, and I've no intention of reminding anyone about that mess."

Grace's shoulders drooped slightly at this, noticing her mother's expression still curled with distaste at the word *elopement*. Still, she tried to convince herself that just agreeing to be seen in the lodging house was progress, however small.

* * *

"Those tablecloths will be beyond repair by the time this dinner is through," Charles spoke above the sounds of clinking silverware and boisterous proclamations of the food's quality.

Grace sat between the young noble and Edwin with their parents in the row behind them, gazing down from the balcony as the newsboys below devoured what seemed like multiple pounds of food each. Sauces and bits of food were indeed being splattered upon the tablecloths in the boys' eagerness to have their plates and stomachs filled.

"I'm certain their housekeeper will manage," Grace said, before spotting Edith emerge from the kitchen with a few trays of new food for the boys. Edith had not noticed them, what with all her attention on the task of keeping the boys at least somewhat orderly and getting the food and drinks to them. Grace had read accounts of these dinners other years, so she knew it was important to keep up with the boys, providing new servings as fast as they could clear the dishes or else risk complete chaos from the hungry throng. It was no wonder Edith had no time to spare a glance up at the balcony of onlookers. Henry had welcomed everyone to the dinner and led the boys in their prayers, but Grace did not think he had spotted his in-laws amidst the crowds of people either.

"But why waste such finery on a band of street peddlers?" Charles asked.

"All in the Christmas spirit," Mr. Dunn answered. "Alms for the poor and such. And these poor boys at least are trying to provide for themselves by working selling newspapers."

"You might provide them with the food in a more fitting setting though," Charles replied.

Mr. Dunn seemed at a loss as to how to answer that. "This is the more democratic way," Grace supplied. "Regardless of their position, they have the potential to be successful and so are entitled to the same fine dining experience any other American might expect for Christmas."

"It is quite interesting," Sir John replied. "Though I cannot imagine anything like this happening in Europe. We give alms and money for charities, of course, but providing the impoverished with the same finery as more civilized society is another thing entirely."

Grace caught the slight frown that tugged at her mother's lips as she glanced away in thought. She could not help but wonder if her mother was recalling what she had said in the toy store. They continued to watch the rest of dinner in silence. It was not until the final courses were being served that Grace spotted Thomas talking animatedly with three other newsboys she assumed were the friends he had mentioned. When the dinner was over, they bid farewell to the Fitzsimmonses in a somewhat more reserved manner than Grace thought her parents had greeted them with.

As the family gathered up their coats and hats, Grace noticed Edwin draping his jacket over his arm rather than putting it on and taking a few steps nearer to their parents. "You know, I've been thinking, and it might be a rather good idea to pop in downstairs. Just to give Edith a quick greeting."

"Your father and I realize that you and Edith are close, dear," Mrs. Dunn replied, resolutely fastening the buttons of her thick coat. "But she has embarrassed the family with her elopement and so she must accept the consequences."

"It's just I've been hearing that quite a few people find elopement stories to be 'romantic' and rather thrilling." Edwin continued calmly. "So it might do some good to be seen trying to make amends. I don't mean anything drastic, of course," he added hastily when Mr. Dunn opened his mouth to comment on the suggestion. "But there is no harm in stopping in to wish her and her husband a merry Christmas."

"Edwin does have a point," Grace piped up as she realized what he was trying to do. "Quite the modern-minded thing to do, don't you think? A show of goodwill during the Christmas season despite any unpleasantness, rather than being so old-fashioned as to ignore a family member altogether." Remembering her mother's behavior when Sir John mentioned how things were done in Europe, she hoped this argument would cut through her lingering anger at Edith. She watched as Mrs. Dunn frowned in thought, glancing between her two children and the remaining figures downstairs.

"You did say declaring that we were cutting all ties to her could put us in a bad light," Mrs. Dunn said, turning to her husband. "Being seen to still be cordial might just make the story less of a scandal."

So with a quick nod from Mr. Dunn it was decided, and they began heading toward the stairs. Busy helping the lodging house staff clear away the places the boys had left, though a few remained in their seats apparently too full to move, Edith did not notice them approaching until they were just a few feet away.

"Oh, goodness," she stammered, eyes wide with disbelief as she shifted the plates she had gathered into one hand and she subconsciously reached up to push away the strands of hair that had fallen out of place during the night. "I didn't think you would...I mean, I never looked..."

"It was a rather spontaneous decision to come," Mr. Dunn explained. "It is Christmas, after all."

"Oh, Father," Edith spoke, and Grace caught the hint of excitement in her voice. "I'm so very glad you did. I really do miss you all. Though you must understand," she added, her voice turning just a little more serious as she made eye contact with each of her parents.

"I love Henry, I'm happier with him than I could be with any other man."

"We do understand," her father replied. "As Grace mentioned during the dinner, Americans do things the democratic way, and this place and your marrying the man of your choice is what democracy is about."

"Even if it is not quite what we hoped for you," her mother added, "it is a shame to leave a rift in the family over the matter. And you and Henry deserve commendation for what you've done for these children."

"Oh, but it can go so much further than just one dinner," Edith replied. "Would you care to come to our apartment? The staff is so efficient here; they've practically cleared everything already," she added, glancing around just as a waiter approached them, having noticed that company had arrived he offered to take the dishes Edith had collected. "I've been reading all about new ideas for a true democracy, perhaps you would be interested."

With only a little reluctance, the family followed Edith out of the dining room. As they passed one table, Grace noticed Thomas's friends had apparently left though he was only just rising from his seat.

"Thomas," she said, "would you like to join us? I'm sure Edith wouldn't mind, and you mustn't be left alone on Christmas."

He seemed surprised by the offer, but he had admitted to her that he had few people he could share the holidays with. After a moment his expression returned to its normal casual smile. "If the rest of your family don't object, then I'd be happy to join." So with that, the two went to catch up with the group.

They made their way to the superintendent's apartment just as Grace's family was stepping inside. Noticing Grace coming along, Edith held the door open. She smiled when she saw Thomas a step behind her sister, though there was a hint of confusion in her eyes.

"Thomas has not made any other Christmas plans," Grace spoke up, "so I thought he might join us for a little while. If that is all right, that is," she added, a hint of a question in her voice. It had felt so natural to invite Thomas along when she saw him sitting at that table all alone, she hadn't even taken a moment to really think about it before the words had been out of her mouth. But now that she was looking at her family she found herself doubting her decision. What if Edith and Henry wanted to retain a professional relationship with the newsboys? After all, even if her sister was living much more simply than she had before her marriage, she was still so obviously different from any of the boys in her care. Her apron might have a few smears of icing and drops of cider and other remains from the meal she served, but underneath was a dress that looked fairly new and well-cared for. Thomas, on the other hand, wore a plain vest for the occasion. It looked cleaner than the coat she had seen him in all the other times but still seemed a bit faded and looked a size or so too big for him.

"Of course," Edith replied, allowing Grace to feel a rush of relief. "It is Christmas, after all. We can't very well leave anyone on their own. Come in, Thomas." Edith smiled wide, stepping aside and gesturing them in to where the family were already settling in on the chairs and sofa.

Spin a Yarn

I sit down at the spinning wheel
Learning to spin flax into linen.
The pointed spindle standing tall
Sparking memories of a childhood tale,
Of a slighted fairy's vengeance.
I set to work.
My foot slowly presses the pedal
As my fingers guide twisting yellow fibers.

"Gather round my little ones."
A grandmother sits by the hearth,
Her foot on the pedal beats a steady rhythm.
And the wheel turning with a gentle hum
Just like Fortuna's wheel.
"And I'll tell you a tale."

Awkwardly I pull strands from the distaff.
The flax rough against my fingertips
As my foot struggles to keep a steady pace
And suddenly the three crones,
Foot, finger, and lip swollen and calloused
Become easy to imagine.
Always something wrong.
Too many strands come down
Tarnishing previously spun thread.
I take a breath,
Patience. Patience.
Like Cinderella
Working and waiting for her chance;
And Sleeping Beauty's Prince
Who pushed onward against each task.

I tear away the mess.
And start again.

"Higher and higher the valiant prince climbed,
to reach his flaxen haired lover."
The children's wide eyes are locked on her
They can almost see beautiful Rapunzel's locks
As she draws down more fiber.
Her voice, shifting between laughter, sorrow, and triumph,
Joined with the rhythm of the wheel
And the crackle of the fire.
Children entranced, pulled in to a story
Just like the whirling bobbin draws freshly spun thread.
Her words weaving pictures in young minds
Of ancient legends from their past,
Older even than the big tree outside,
With walnuts that will give new clothes their color.
She teases their imaginations
With far off places
More exotic than the lands
Where indigo and other richer hues are found.

Even as I struggle,
There are moments,
Mere seconds really,
When I see it
A half-imagined glint of gold
Instead of simple thread.
Loose flax, looking so much like straw
Becoming solid and strong.
And as I learn a spinster's craft
I discover the seeds of inspiration
For the storyteller's art.

Sleepless Nights

Snowflakes danced in the chill breeze outside the window, swirling and spinning through the air to settle on the ground. The thin layer of snow already settled on the ground made the light of the full moon seem even brighter as it shone through the linen curtains. Sybil would likely be closing the shutters of her own bedchamber, but she knew her grandsons were uneasy without a little bit of light at night. The fireplace continued to burn in the parlor where her son reviewed his recent cases and law books, and in the next room over, the newest addition to the family's cries had finally quieted. Which was why Sybil decided to see the boys to bed and give her daughter-in-law a well-deserved rest.

"Couldn't we stay up a little longer, Granny?" Unfortunately, the moonlight was clearly not helping with the concept of bedtime.

"We did all our chores good, didn't we?"

"You did your chores well," she nodded, continuing to usher him into bed now that his toy soldiers were put away. "And that's why you ought to get some sleep."

"But I'm not sleepy at all!" Henry declared, doing a poor job of hiding a yawn but determined to follow his big brother's example. "Couldn't we at least hear a story first?"

"Very well. A story and then you both go to sleep. Do we have a deal?" The boys nodded, settling into the bed. "What sort of story would you like?" she asked, tucking the quilted blanket in around them against any draft.

"Tell us about the war for independence!" Edmund spoke up, not surprisingly considering he had recently been given his father's old set of tin soldiers.

"Did you fight in the war, Granny?" Henry, in all his innocence, asked.

"No, silly," Edmund chided. "Girls don't go to war."

"Oh, they don't, do they?" Sybil replied with a hint of a smile. Certainly, she had plenty of stories of her father's exploits, and though her time with her husband had seemed all too short, he had shared some of his battle experience with her. But the turn the conversation had taken gave her another idea. "Girls may not be expected to go to battle, but sometimes the war would come to us."

"How?"

"Did it come a lot?"

Sybil smiled at the big round eyes now fixed on her. "Quite a lot—and at all hours. I daresay I considered myself lucky if I could lay my head down and get a good long sleep during the war." It was so many years ago, but now as she reached into her memory the days of her girlhood came back as clear as crystal. Leaning back against the Windsor chair beside the boys' bed she let her mind drift back to the Ludington farmhouse of her youth as she began the tale.

* * *

I knew the war would not be easy for anyone and that it would mean many sleepless nights in our household. My brothers and sisters and I were proud when Father was named a colonel in the Continental Army, but that did not mean we were ignorant of the dangers. Fighting against professionally trained soldiers meant going into harm's way. What was more, Father and his regiment were good at it, making a nuisance of themselves at every opportunity. They interrupted supply lines and fended off the Tories that stole cattle from local farms as well as fighting on the battlefield. So naturally, there was a target on him and his men—and our family farm would be right in the midst of it. Still, we were not quite prepared for the lengths British General Howe would go to when Father and his regiment proved a significant obstacle to him. A bounty was placed on Father's head: three hundred English guineas, dead or alive. Fredericksburg, New York, was not like the British-occupied New York City, but there were still some in the area loyal to the crown, especially if they stood to gain such a sum for their services. With that announcement, any hope we had of a quiet life even in the safety of our own home vanished.

I remember the days after news of the reward reached us. The youngest of my siblings were blind to the added dangers it brought. The rest of us, however, remained constantly on edge. So one night, when I heard muffled voices and movement coming from the boys' bedroom, my mind instantly imagined some attacker in the house. I leapt out of the bed, barely hearing Mary's frantic questions of what was happening. I noticed Rebecca having the same reaction as I did, already half out of the opposite side of our bed. However, with Mary clutching at her sleeve, she stayed to try and calm the eleven-year-old.

I burst into the boys' chamber, my heart in my throat with panic. All four boys were still in the bed they shared but all were awake. Henry Jr. was the first to catch my attention. The eight-year-old's paler than usual skin almost glowed like snow in the moonlight and strands of fair hair stuck to his forehead, damp with sweat. He sat in the center of the bed, his arms clasped tightly around himself. All eyes had turned to me the moment I entered the room but while the others seemed either still half asleep or mildly annoyed, his were wide and fearful.

"Sorry to wake you, Sybil," Archibald spoke up. "But Henry Jr. was having a bad dream, and he was kicking a lot. Between that and me trying to wake him up..." he trailed off without finishing the explanation, but I could guess what happened from there. The commotion woke the others and led to surprise and confusion.

"It's all right. Just try and get back to sleep," I said. I was about to turn and leave when I noticed that while Tertullus and Derick nestled back into their pillows eager to follow the advice, Henry Jr. remained in exactly the same position.

"He'll stay like that for a while," Archibald said, noticing my questioning look. "He always does after a nightmare."

"You've been having them a lot, lately?" I asked Henry Jr., taking a few steps into the room. He simply gave a small nod. "Do you want to talk about it?"

"Just a dream," he murmured, sapphire eyes flitting up to the ceiling where we could hear a faint creak. Henry Jr. should have known as well as I that it was just Mother or Father moving about. Perhaps walking around the room with Little Abby to get her back to sleep. And yet there was something odd in his expression as his gaze fixed on the source of the sound.

"Very well," I replied. "Then why not just lie down and try to get some sleep? Staying awake so long shan't do you any good," I added, remembering the dark circles under his eyes I had noticed over the past few days. Even with the full moon shining through the window, it was too dark to see such details now, but it was obvious enough that this was the reason behind them.

Henry Jr. shook his head, remaining sitting up even as the other boys were closing their eyes ready for sleep. However, before I could insist anymore, light footsteps echoed from the ceiling. I recognized Father's stride, barefoot and attempting to step softly, but still purposeful and firm. The footsteps moved to the front of the house and descended the staircase. Soon enough, Father was coming down the hall to join me by the doorway. He held a small candlestick that replaced the soft silvery moonlight with a pool of bright gold.

"I thought I heard voices down here," Father said, glancing around at us. "Is everything all right?"

"Yes, Henry Jr. had a bad dream, and I came in to see what was going on," I explained. As I spoke I glanced over at Henry Jr. and noticed his demeanor had changed. His arms now lay relaxed at his side, and his gaze was focused on Father. I thought I saw a hint of relief in his expression.

"I see," Father said before turning to Henry Jr. "It must have been quite the nightmare to have woken you and your siblings."

Henry Jr. gave a small nod, glancing down as his fingers traced the stitches of the quilt. "It was a bit...well, I...I'm all right now. I-I think I can try to sleep now."

"All right," Father said, watching Henry Jr. slide under the blanket. "Sleep well, boys. Thank you for checking on them, Sybil, but you'd best get some sleep as well."

I nodded, following Father out of the room. I wished him and the boys good night as I closed the door behind us before returning to my own room. Rebecca and Mary had apparently been able to hear enough of the conversation from across the hall to realize it was nothing serious. Mary was already drifting back to sleep, barely stirring as I climbed into bed beside her. Rebecca was lying down but decidedly more awake than our younger sister.

"One of them had a bad dream?" she whispered.

"Henry Jr. Archibald says he's had quite a few lately," I replied, keeping my voice just as low.

"Hardly surprising," she replied, rolling onto her side and propping her head up, looking at me over Mary's head. "Everyone has been tense lately. We both feared the worst when we heard the noise."

"He would not say, but I think it had something to do with the bounty. Even awake, he looked terrified until Father came in."

"Night always feels like the most vulnerable time." Rebecca's voice grew even quieter than it already was.

Mary's slow, even breathing, and her reputation for falling asleep quickly, made me fairly sure she was already asleep, but I still lowered my voice as well. "Yes, at least during the day, there is enough activity around the farm that someone should notice if something is amiss."

Just then, there was a faint creaking sound that caused Rebecca and I to stiffen. We lay in silence for a few seconds before I finally realized it was just the sound of the wind against the shutters of the window. Relaxing, I released a breath I hadn't realized I was holding and the soft sigh on the other side of the bed told me Rebecca had done the same.

"It might be a little easier if we could go to sleep knowing there's no Tories lurking in the woods just waiting for the last candle to be blown out," I murmured.

"You know, I think you're right," Rebecca replied slowly. "There would still be the chance of them coming late in the night. But if we could check on the property before we went to sleep…at least it would be something."

"Like a patrol?" I replied, an idea beginning to form in my mind. "Just around the house wouldn't do much good. We'd want to know the outbuildings and fields were clear."

"I suppose," Rebecca replied. I heard a soft rustle of the sheets as if she shrugged. "But there's no point in Father doing it. If there were bounty hunters out there, it would be like handing him over to them, and the boys are too young to manage such a thing."

I did not answer right away. I had already thought of both those points, which left only one other choice. However, as clear as the solution was, there was also sure to be resistance to it.

"What if…" I hesitated, fighting to speak despite feeling like my stomach was tying itself in knots. "What if you and I patrolled the farm?"

"Us?" Rebecca asked incredulously. "Two girls? We wouldn't…I mean…how could we—"

"We both know how to use a rifle," I interrupted, already knowing what she was thinking. I, myself, was a little surprised to be even suggesting such a thing. It was one thing for Father to teach us how to use a rifle as a precaution against raids or Loyalist violence while he and his regiment were elsewhere. It was another matter entirely to consider actively looking for potential threats. Rather than listen to Rebecca repeat my own misgivings aloud, I had to focus on why we should try.

"The point would be to have forewarning, not seek out a fight. Just around our own family's property. What harm could it do? More importantly what harm could come if we don't?"

There was silence for a moment. "Do you…do you think Father would allow it?"

We spent a few more minutes discussing ways we might try to convince our parents. As we spoke, I was still nervous, hardly believing we were seriously considering patrolling like sentries. But the more we discussed it, the more confident I felt that it would be worth it. War put everyone in difficult positions, and we had to do what we could to keep our loved ones safe.

We agreed to try to talk to Mother and Father without any of our siblings around. Neither of them were going to be thrilled with the idea, so getting into a debate over the issue in front of the younger ones would only make things more difficult. The next morning, Rebecca volunteered to help Mother clear the table after breakfast as our siblings went off to their own chores. Meanwhile, I mentioned that we could use more logs on-hand in the kitchen, knowing Father would join me to fetch some from the woodpile outside so we could manage it in one trip.

Once Father and I returned to the kitchen with an armful of wood each, I wasted no time in telling them about our late night conversation. And, as expected, it was not greeted with enthusiasm.

"Sybil, marching about with rifles on your shoulders is hardly appropriate for two young ladies," Mother replied firmly. Shaking off her initial shock at the suggestion as she began returning plates to the cupboard.

"But Mother, you must admit this would be a great help," I insisted, knowing she was just as worried about Father as we were. She too always grew tense whenever there was a knock at the door or unknown sound. "There is no one else to do it. Father would be their target to begin with, and Archibald is only just learning to handle a rifle. Besides, I am fifteen—early sixteen—the same age you were when you married, and Rebecca is just two years younger. If you could start a family at the same age, why shouldn't we be old enough to protect ours?"

Mother gave a small sigh as she shut the cupboard. She looked first at Rebecca and I before her gaze shifted to Father who was finishing stacking the logs we had brought in. "What do you think, Henry?"

I knew Father would be the hardest to convince but decided to wait patiently for his response rather than continue pressing the matter for now. Mother shared our worry and sense of helplessness, so all we had to do was make her see that the dangers of war were warranted a break with propriety. Once that point was out of the way she would soon agree that our idea was better than doing nothing. Father on the other hand, would initially see it as being asked to hide behind his children, and daughters at that, which would be completely out of the question.

Father stared thoughtfully at the flames in the hearth. A moment after the flames began to crawl along the splintered end of one log, he straightened and fixed his bright blue eyes on mine. "I appreciate your concern girls, and it is very brave of you both to volunteer this idea. However, I can't allow you or anyone in this family to take such a risk for my sake."

"But Father, if bounty hunters come here, all of us will be in danger," I replied. Our only hope was to convince him that these patrols would be a means of protecting our family as much as it was about protecting him. "You can't honestly expect us to just step aside if Tories come bursting in, intending to turn you over to Howe. And even if we did, there is no guarantee they would stop with you. They may start shooting at every window or even burn the whole house down."

"Sybil, the little ones are just in the next room," Mother chided. I had started out intent to keep a level head, making rational arguments, but my nerves had left me agitated, and my voice had been rising a bit more than intended.

"We want to protect them from the war as much as you do," Rebecca chimed in. "But we have all heard about our neighbors who have lost their homes and even been attacked simply because of which side they chose. You know there is a good chance that such things could happen to us. And if it comes to that, there will be no protecting anyone in this house from what war means."

"Rebecca is right," I said, having regained my composure as Rebecca spoke. Ever since news of the bounty reached us, I had noticed Father fall into serious moods more often. He never showed worry, but something was different. He focused on plans for the farm, his gristmill, and his regiment when he used to pause to playfully inspect the way Derick or Henry Jr. had arranged their toy soldiers or any of the other little things he did with my siblings and I. He still took me along when he went to check in with the men of his regiment or make sure that things at his gristmill was running smoothly, but he seemed distracted and somber. We used to talk idly about anything that came to mind, but recently, he seemed to be listening to every sound of the woods around us instead of making conversation. Perhaps it was, in part, from worry for his own safety, but I thought he could have suppressed the signs of that fear more thoroughly. Father knew any attempt to kill or capture him while with us would put his family in danger, so perhaps a reminder of that would help to change his mind.

"It's true most of us did not really worry much before General Howe's reward," I continued, "but we live in the no-man's land. The truth is there have been dangers ever since the war began. Even without your appointment as colonel or the reward, we would still be vulnerable to attacks from Cowboys; even turncoat Skinners who didn't find enough travelers to ambush could very well decide to raid our fields or barn." Men known as Cowboys and Skinners had been roaming the woods in our area since the beginning of the war. Officially, Cowboys aided the British, stealing cattle and provisions to deliver to the Redcoats, and Skinners helped the Patriots, but both were known to change sides, depending on what offered the greatest profit. Generally, it was best to avoid both groups whenever possible. Regardless of whichever title they claimed, the people of Fredericksburg had come to consider the majority of them as no better than thieves. They took whatever they pleased from their victims as they had been known to claim to suspect any travelers as an excuse to rob them. Attacks on people's property were less frequent, but it was still known to happen, whether by Cowboys and Skinners, soldiers camped nearby, or even just angry neighbors.

Father remained silent for a moment, standing tall, his jaw set in a firm line that revealed nothing about the thoughts going through his mind. Finally, he gave a small sigh as he reached some conclusion.

"If you are both sure you're willing to take on this task, I will allow it, on two conditions," he added. The commanding tone of the last words made it obvious that they would not be negotiable. Rebecca and I remained silent waiting to see what he would demand. "You will both carry a loaded hunting rifle during these patrols. However, you are not to use them unless you have absolutely no other choice. If you see anything amiss, however small, you are to come straight back to the house as quickly as possible and inform me."

Rebecca and I looked to each other just to be sure we were both in agreement. She wore a hint of a smile with a determined look in her eyes that I suspected mirrored my own.

"Agreed," we replied. Neither of us really wanted to take on any bounty hunters ourselves, even if we might be willing to take the risk for our family's sake. In truth, we hoped the patrols would prove unnecessary; they would just be a way to help put our minds at ease.

And that was all it was for the first months. Rebecca and I patrolled around the house, fields, orchard, and outbuildings with nothing more threatening than a fox darting away from us into the shelter of the woods. However, as winter began, enduring the long walks and dropping temperatures proved to be well worthwhile. By that time, we were not quite so anxious as we had been the first few nights, but we still never talked very much. We wanted to remain focused on our task and not become too relaxed with idle chatter. So we were making our way silently alongside our small apple orchard when the sound of a snapping twig broke through the cool night air. Rebecca and I froze for a moment before edging into the shade of the apple trees, grateful for our dark-colored cloaks. We squinted into the woods that stood just beyond the orchard where the sound had come from. I tried to tell myself it was probably just an animal in the wood, with little success. As we now stood, straining for a noise or glimpse of something, I could make out the barely audible rustling of dry leaves that littered the ground in the woods across from our home. Then, I spotted the distinct shapes of men passing through the moonlit space created by a gap in the canopy. My heart clenched as I took in the sight. They were only silhouettes and difficult to distinguish one from another as they walked so closely together, but it was painfully clear that there were too many of them and the hour too late to mean anything but a sizable band of bounty hunters.

I felt Rebecca's hand clamp around my arm. "Are those rifles?" Her voice was nothing more than a whisper, but I still heard the tremble in her voice. I nodded, my gaze fixed on the long shadows that protruded above a few of the tri-cornered heads that had to be hunting rifles. The fact that we both recognized the weapons so easily, even just by the silhouettes, struck me with an idea that transformed all my fear into a focused determination.

"Come on, I have a plan," I whispered, tugging Rebecca's arm as I moved toward the house before tightly clutching my rifle with both hands. We quickly wove through the apple trees; my toes catching the hem of my skirt once or twice, but I couldn't hold the rifle securely with one hand to lift it. Fortunately, my everyday petticoat was getting a little short on me so as long as I concentrated on my steps I avoided actually tripping. The men would surely be headed for the door of the house which meant from the direction they were coming they would have a perfect view of the parlor windows as they approached. So that was where I would put my plan in motion. Despite our hurry I dared not risk any sound that might alert the bounty hunters that they had been spotted, fearing it might spur them to action faster. So as I reached the house, I slowly opened the door just wide enough to pass through before gesturing for Rebecca to slip inside and following close behind.

"Go tell Father what we saw. We'll need everyone in the parlor right away," I told Rebecca as I gently closed the door again, sliding the bolt firmly in place though I hoped they'd never reach the door. By the time I had set the rifle down, Rebecca was already halfway up the stairs toward Mother and Father's chamber.

"Oh! And tell the boys to bring all their toy rifles as well," I added. This earned a quizzical look thrown over her shoulder, but Rebecca thankfully was not going to waste time asking questions in such a situation.

Meanwhile, I darted into the kitchen and made my way to the cabinet and flung the doors open. I began grabbing every candlestick I could see, from the finest silver candlesticks for special occasions to the simple iron taper holders. Once I had as many as I could carry in my arms I heard footsteps behind me and turned to see Archibald.

"I heard you and Rebecca coming in," he said. "What's going on? And what are you doing with all those candlesticks?"

"I'll explain in a minute," I replied, the breathless sound of my own voice forcing me to notice how hard my heart was pounding. "Grab as many candles as you can from the milk room," I added, before hurrying past my brother and into the parlor realizing that I would not be able to manage carrying the candles in addition to the candlesticks already in my grasp. Mother, Father, and Rebecca were coming down the stairs just as I was passing it to get to the parlor.

Father, unsurprisingly, had brought the rifle that he always kept on hand ever since the war started. Unlike the ones Rebecca and I used, it could have a bayonet attached and so was useful for close fighting as well as firing on opponents. Rebecca did not miss a step, gripping the end of the banister as she swung herself around it and headed to the back of the house to summon our siblings.

"Sybil, we do have more effective weapons than candlesticks," Father said, as he and Mother followed me into the parlor. I could tell he was trying to lighten the situation with humor, but I was too focused on organizing my plan to bother following his example.

"The only thing that could stand a chance against that many men is a whole regiment," I replied. I dropped the candlesticks unceremoniously on the sofa before turning to the nearest window and roughly pulling the linen curtains closed. Belatedly, I hoped none of the candlesticks, particularly the silver ones, had been damaged when I dropped them. The fact that Mother was not scolding me already was proof of how anxious she was about the bounty hunters. I quickly glanced around the room at all the candles already in sconces along the wall. Most seemed too low to last the whole night so I began blowing them out and removing the candles. Just then, Archibald wove around Mother and Father with his arms laden with candles.

"Start putting those fresh candles in place, would you, Archibald?" I said. He set to the task without a word just as Rebecca led our other siblings into the room as well.

"Sybil, those Tories are right outside the house. How exactly do you intend to get a regiment of men here to stop them?" Mother asked, struggling to keep the panic we all felt from showing in her voice.

"I intend to make them think the men are already here," I replied, pulling the last curtain shut as I passed the window. "We are going to march around the parlor, just like we've all watched Father's men do when they muster here, carrying rifles. Through the curtains those Tories will only see our shadows, if we keep close enough they won't be able to pick out details, but they will see there are many of us and each one carrying something that looks like a rifle." I nodded toward the carved wooden toys Henry Jr. and Derrick were carrying as well as the real weapons in Rebecca's arms as she came into the room after scooping up my rifle.

With that, I began taking up the candlesticks and positioning them on the mantle and nearby tables for Archibald to put fresh candles in. Father took up a tall candle I had left in the sconce and began lighting each of the new candles as soon as Archibald had secured it in place.

"Mary, Rebecca, go and fetch the boxes in the weaving room for the little ones to walk on," Mother instructed. Too busy rushing to set up the candles, I had not thought of the height problem. Archibald and Henry Jr., who both inherited Father's height, might pass for young or rather short soldiers. However, at six and four years old, Derick and Tertullus would never convince anyone unless they marched on a raised surface. Thankfully, Mother had a talent for thinking clearly under pressure and had foreseen this challenge.

"Henry Jr., come with me upstairs," Mother added before hurrying toward the staircase with Henry Jr. close behind.

"Soldiers would be wearing their shoes if they were guarding the house," Father called over his shoulder as he continued lighting candles. With that, Derick darted off to gather shoes for everyone who had taken them off preparing to go to sleep.

Just as we finished setting the candles in place and arranging the boxes Rebecca and Mary had brought in, Mother and Henry Jr. appeared in the parlor carrying Father's uniform coat, greatcoat, hunting frock, and linen jacket. Mother quickly passed these out amongst Mary, Rebecca, and I and began putting one on herself, explaining that it would disguise our figures and give our silhouettes the shape of uniformed soldiers—or at least, what militiamen usually wore. The boys remained in their own clothes since it was not that uncommon for soldiers to wear only their shirts or perhaps a smaller coat especially while indoors.

Moments later, we had arranged the boxes on the floor in the middle of the room. Tertullus, Derick, and Henry Jr. would march on top of them forming one line while Father, Archibald, and I marched nearest the parlor windows and Rebecca, Mother, and Mary formed

the last line against the far wall. We aligned ourselves in a staggered pattern instead of being lined up to the shoulder of the "soldier" next to us as we marched back and forth. Rebecca had pointed out that this might create the illusion of an even larger group. Each of the boys carried their toy guns, Father had his own rifle, and Rebecca and I took up the ones we carried on our patrols. Being used to the weight, we would be more likely to hold them correctly than the others who handled real guns far less often. Mary held a piece of wood that Mother had been planning to use as a broom handle, and Mother carried a poker from the fire with the point facing down so as to stay closer to the shape of a rifle.

We marched back and forth across the parlor like that for hours, letting our feet fall heavily to the floor. I prayed we would look and sound like well-trained soldiers, accustomed to long nights of marching, rather than children who were up considerably past their bedtime. Little Abby woke up only once during the night and began crying. Mother had to slip out of the formation, waiting until she was sure she was out of sight from all the windows, and go upstairs to soothe her. Thankfully, Mother's experience with raising seven children before Abby meant it took her no time at all to calm her, and soon the cries faded as she drifted back to sleep. Soon enough, Mother had slipped seamlessly back into formation.

None of us dared to peek through the curtains to see if the bounty hunters were approaching the house or not. I desperately wanted to; it would be so easy to just brush aside the curtain an inch and take a quick look. But if the Tories were close enough, they might notice a girl's face looking out—especially with the room so brightly lit—and grow suspicious of our charade. Even if one of the boys looked, if the men were local Tories, they might recognize one of my brothers, and if they recognized Father, they might just take the opportunity to fire at him and collect their reward. Instead, we all just continued to march in perfect formation and simply hoped to hear something that might give us some clue as to what the bounty hunters were doing. As anxious as having no clear sign about their intentions made me, I tried to tell myself that only hearing the steady beat of my family's footsteps on the floorboards was a good sign. I

meant no one was firing at the house or trying to force their way through the door at the very least.

So instead, I let my gaze move over the room, still listening for any clue outside but looking for something to occupy my thoughts for the time being. Derick caught my eye as he turned at the end of the box path. Those blue eyes, the same color as Father's, shining with excitement as his small shoulders were held perfectly squared and straight despite the late hour and weight of the wooden toy resting on one shoulder. Barely in breeches for a year, and he already thought himself ready for the life of a soldier. Clearly, the five-year-old had no doubts that this plan would work. Perhaps he thought this was just a more exciting version of all the times he spent herding our sheep as he pretended to be a colonel of his own regiment. Tertullus was looking groggy, but he apparently was aware enough of how serious we all were not to complain aloud about how much I'm sure he wanted to be in bed. The rest of us, including myself, remained somber and alert, too anxious to realize our own drowsiness.

It was not until the sun was beginning to rise, its dull light just peeking through the curtains, that we agreed it would be safe to stop our performance. Father was the first to draw the curtain aside, glancing around to see if there was any sign of the bounty hunters. "Looks clear," he said letting the curtain drop back into place.

"So we frightened them off?" Derick asked.

"I'll take a look around the property to be sure," Father said, already turning toward the door.

"But Father," I protested. He was the one they had come for in the first place; surely he would not risk going out while they still might be here. "If they're out there and see you they—"

"If they have been out in the cold for an entire night, they will be in no mood to spare anyone that happens upon them," Father cut my protestations off. His voice was gentle, but I knew the tone that meant his decision was made. "Especially if they believe there is an entire regiment in this house who will descend upon them in moments if they allow anyone to raise the alarm. I agreed to you and Rebecca making patrols because it would help prevent any danger to

everyone. I will not allow any of you to take such risks solely on my account."

When the rest of us remained silent, he turned and made his way out the door. I was thankful that he took his weapon but still felt nervous.

After that, Mother quickly set everyone to their morning chores. I knew she hoped it would provide at least a small distraction from thoughts of whether or not the bounty hunters had left. We were all beginning to feel rather drowsy, but Mother insisted we have our morning meal and accomplish at least a few of our daily chores before resting. I was setting the table when Father came through the door. Instantly, all of us were rushing into the hall.

"They're long gone," he said confidently. "I found the spot where they must have been watching the house for a time, judging by worn down undergrowth, but the trail shows them going away from the property. Their position would have had a clear view of the south window," he added with a smile in my direction. "Sybil's idea seems to have worked perfectly."

"Hopefully, they assume some men are guarding the house all the time," Archibald replied, his words followed by an only partially stifled yawn.

"Yes, it would be a shame if we had to stay awake every night just to send a bunch of Tories back to their own comfortable beds," Father replied, affectionately tousling Archibald's hair and earning a small chuckle from the boy. "Now! I can smell your Mother's cooking, and I'm sure you're all as hungry as I am after a full night of soldiering."

With that we all filed into the kitchen finishing the last of the table settings and food that needed preparing. After breakfast, Mother still insisted on a few chores getting done but did not scold anyone who took a little longer than normal, and by noon, all of us had taken at least a short break to nap between our tasks. Rebecca and I still patrolled again that night, determined not to break the habit. Once our rounds were done, we both eagerly climbed into bed and fell asleep almost immediately.

We kept up the patrols after that, but months passed without any real incident. As the year 1777 began, General Washington led the Continental Army to its first major victory. But fighting continued to ravage the colonies. With both armies so close, there was plenty of fighting to keep Father's regiment busy defending our community. It was only a matter of time before we were reminded that the war could strike anywhere at any time.

Rebecca's and my patrol on April 26 was a rather unpleasant one as it started to rain toward the end of our rounds. We were both relieved to return to the house once we had completed the route. My shoes had a fresh coat of mud along their bottoms, forcing me to take them off at the door rather than track it through the house. It would be easier to clean them when the mud was dry in the morning. After peeking into the boys' room to see they were all in bed, I went to the kitchen to sweep up. Rebecca went to blow out the candles in the parlor. I knew Mother would be upstairs with Little Abby by this time and the flicker of candle light coming from the sitting room showed where Father was, most likely working on plans for the farm now that the planting season had begun. Once the kitchen was completely tidy, I went to my bedchamber. Mary was already nestled under the coverlet though not yet asleep and Rebecca was in her chemise, just climbing into the bed. I was just about to untie the garters of my stockings when there was frantic knocking at the door. Mary sat bolt upright, and Rebecca practically leapt out of the bed as I spun around.

"Stay with Mary," I told Rebecca, not waiting for a response as I rushed out of the room. Memories of shadowy figures in the woods and tireless marching through the parlor flashed through my mind. Had we missed something this time? Or had a smaller group moved in during the time it took to finish the chores? Mother came down from the second floor just before I passed the staircase; I could hear the faint sound of Little Abby crying upstairs. Probably woken by the noise and further upset when Mother hurried out of the room rather than soothe her as she normally would.

Father had already opened the door, and he stood in front of a young man. The first thing I noticed was the stranger's posture.

His shoulders were slumped, and he was breathing heavily, not the stance of an assassin. The tightness in my chest eased, though every muscle remained tense. Beside me, Mother seemed to relax as well, though her eyes never left the man in the doorway. He was completely drenched from the rain. He could only have stepped inside a second ago, but there was already a puddle forming around his feet.

Despite how exhausted he was the man wasted no time to reveal his purpose here. "Colonel Ludington," he panted, "the Redcoats… they're burning Danbury!"

Father gave a curt nod and gestured for the man to follow him to the parlor and dry off by the fire. We all followed them and watched as he collapsed in the wooden chair beside the fireplace as Father stirred the embers back to life and placed a fresh log over them. The man was still breathing heavily, and his muddied clothes were torn in a few places, suggesting he had been riding hard through the thickly wooded paths. Father looked from the messenger to the fire, deep in thought. I knew why such news was so distressing to him. The idea of a city being burned was terrible enough, but this was an especially difficult time for it to happen. Most of Father's men were farmers, so he had given them all leave to begin planting and managing their fields. That meant they were all scattered throughout Fredericksburg and the surrounding areas. Riding out to gather them himself was not an option. Father had to be at our house and ready to lead them the moment they all arrived if there was to be any chance of saving Danbury. There was only one option I could think of. Taking a deep breath and trying not to think of the dangers I took a step forward.

"I'll go, Father," I said firmly. I knew if I showed any hint of fear Father would be even less comfortable with the idea.

"Sybil, it's dangerous," Mother said, placing her hand on my shoulder.

"I've gone with you to the men's houses often enough. I know the quickest routes," I persisted, not taking my eyes off of Father's face.

"That was in the daytime and with me," Father replied. His stoic manner made it impossible for me to guess whether he was at least considering the suggestion. "The woods could be full of Cowboys, not to mention natural dangers."

"I doubt they will be very active in this storm," I said. In truth, I really had no idea if the weather would deter the bandits, but I hoped it would. "Besides, there is no other option. You must be here to meet the men if you are to reach the British in time. Archibald is too young for such a ride, and this gentleman is in no state to ride again."

Father paused a moment as we made eye contact. I held his gaze not letting myself think of anything other than how this had to be done for our country. It probably only took him a few seconds to decide though it felt like hours as we were all painfully aware that time was precious if he was to do anything to help Danbury.

"Get a cloak and hat," he instructed. "I'll have Star ready for you outside."

Everything after that went by so fast. I remember Mother fastening my cloak as I tied a broad-brimmed hat under my chin. Then Mother was giving me a tight embrace, filling my nose with the faint scent of lavender that was always around her and the fresh bread we had made earlier in the day.

"Be careful, sweetheart," she said, gently touching the edge of the hat. It was a habit she had ever since I was little. The result of always adjusting the clothes of my siblings and I before we left the house to make sure we would stay warm and dry or protected from the sun. She had not done it to me though in a long time. "Come home safe."

"I will, Mother," I promised, "once the men are rallied." After that, I hurried out the door and to the stable. The raindrops fell so hard I could feel the impact even through my cloak as I ran toward the stable. I braced myself for the hardest journey I had ever made and silently vowed to give my horse, Star, some extra treats for the next week for what I was going to put her through. I helped Father finish saddling Star and was in the saddle the second everything was ready. Father reached out, his strong hand on my arm stopped me from spurring Star into action.

"I know you can do this, just be careful," he said. He must have known Mother would say something like that, too, but I suppose he felt he needed to as well. I nodded and gave what I hoped was a confident smile. With an encouraging squeeze, he let go of my arm and I was off, urging Star on at full speed. The rain soaked through my cloak, and continued to seep down through my gown and shift. I was riding faster than I ever tried before and still it seemed to take too long. All I could think about was Danbury in flames, and Father counting on me to get his men to him in time to help fight the Redcoats off.

With rain clouds shrouding the moon, I was glad I had so often joined Father traveling the area while he was visiting the men in his regiment. Otherwise the paths would have been impossible to follow in these conditions. Knowing the first house would soon be in sight, I broke a thin but sturdy branch that hung low in my path. When I came to the first house, I rode up to the wooden fence that surrounded an herb garden at the side of the house and began hitting one of the posts with my stick. The vibrations of the impact traveled from the stick all the way up my arm but I needed to rouse the house quickly.

"Wake up! You're needed!" I shouted until a window opened revealing the shadowed shape of a child. "The Redcoats are in Danbury, 'tis burning!" I screamed over the wind not bothering to determine which of the family's children I had woken. "Tell your father to go to the Ludington farm straight away!" There was a pause as the drowsy child seemed unable to take in the instructions. "Go fetch him, quickly! To the Ludington farm!"

The tiny figure moved as if nodding and rushed out of sight. Content that my instructions would be followed, I was off again with a flick of the rains, urging Star back to full speed.

I had already made it to a few of the houses, shouting the news of Danbury and telling the men to muster at the Ludington farm. However, as I thought over the route between all the men's farms I realized stopping at every house myself would be foolish. Scattered throughout the area a stop at each would require me to detour and double back so many times I could never reach all the houses in time. In fact, the Baker farm was next on my route, but after that, I there was one more house to the north but nearly all the others lay to the west. With that thought, I made my decision.

I rode up to a tree that stood near the Baker family's farmhouse before sliding out of Star's saddle. I was thankful that she was well enough trained to not wander off, especially since the tree at least gave her partial shelter from the rain. I quickly pounded on the Dutch door, waiting anxiously for someone to open it, unable to hear if footsteps were approaching the door over the rain that beat down on the wooden roof. Finally, the top half of the door swung open to reveal the tall broad shouldered figure of Mr. Baker.

"Sybil? What are you—"

"The British are burning Danbury," I spoke up, I knew my arrival in the middle of the night would be a surprise to all the men but there was no time to waste on long explanations. "My father is waiting at our home to lead the march there."

It only took him a moment to take in my words. "I'll be there as fast as I can," he said, already moving to close the door and presumably dress and gather everything he would need.

"Ride to the Mead farm first and rouse them," I replied quickly, reaching out to hold the door open causing him to pause. "I need to continue on this route to rally the others."

He gave a quick nod in acknowledgment of the instruction. "God's speed, Sybil," he called after me as I was already making my way back to Star. With that, he shut the door and set about making preparations for his journey and the fight ahead while I mounted Star and returned to my own duty.

"God's speed to us all," I murmured before flicking the reins. I continued on, using the stick and shouting so most of the men only needed to open their windows to see what the commotion was about. This helped to save time as I could shout the instructions and be on my way all the faster. I sent a few more men to wake others that would take me too far out of the way from the rest, but I feared making any man take too great a detour and exhaust themselves or their horses before they even reached the battle. Less fortunately, it was difficult to be heard over the howl of the wind and raindrops pounding against the roof shingles and trees. My throat ached after just a few houses, but I had to keep going.

Forty miles later, the sun was beginning to rise, the rain had lightened at some point on my ride but not before thoroughly soaking me. Now, the sun peeked through the remaining clouds. I'm not sure how long I had been riding, but when my home finally came into sight, all the men were gone. Though the churned up mud was an unmistakable sign that the regiment had all been there. Someone must have been waiting for me by the parlor window because Mother, Rebecca, and Archibald came running out as soon as I slid out of the saddle. I was soaking wet and covered in mud splatter, but Mother did not even tell me to take my shoes off as she ushered me through the door and into the house. Meanwhile, Rebecca and Archibald guided Star to the stable to tend to her. The other children were clustered in the hall. Mother helped me out of my cloak and hung it on one of the pegs near the door.

Tertullus stepped forward the moment I was in the door, eyes wide and alight with a beaming smile. "Sybil, I got to see all of Father's men! Their horses woke me up. And Rebecca said they're going to save Danbury, and I saw the whole thing as they marched off," he told me, bouncing up and down with excitement. I smiled at him; it was a rare occurrence to see the four-year-old pleased to have been woken by anything.

Henry Jr. was on my other side and tugged lightly on my sleeve. "What happened on your ride?"

"It—" I winced, unable to continue as even that single syllable seemed to scratch roughly against my throat.

"Sybil can share stories later," Mary chided the boys as she rocked Little Abby in her arms. Derick stood beside her, groggily rubbing at his eyes; with the initial excitement of this morning's events fading, he seemed to be feeling the effects of the early awakening.

"Come, dear; let's get you out of those wet things and into bed," Mother told me as she guided me toward my bedroom, and Mary ushered the children back into the kitchen. I was grateful for Mother's gentle yet firm arm around my shoulders. My legs were beginning to feel a bit wobbly from such a long time on horseback.

"I'll have breakfast ready soon. Your father wanted you to know he is very proud of you," Mother told me as she helped me remove my soaked and mud covered clothes and change into a new shift. "Now, you've more than earned a good rest."

I climbed into bed, reveling in the inviting softness of the mattress and my feather stuffed pillow.

"So the men got here in time?" I forced out a raspy whisper. Despite the soreness in my throat, I needed to be certain. I eased myself under the blankets, eager for their warmth. I was soaked to the bone and beginning to become aware of the chill. Not to mention the fact that every muscle in my body was protesting how much work I had done in the past few hours.

"Yes, you've done wonderfully," Mother assured me. "Now 'tis up to the men to deal with the British." She kissed my forehead before adding, "Now you're home safe, you needn't worry about anything but resting."

She drew the bed curtains closed, blocking out most of the sunlight, leaving me to fall asleep almost instantly. Later, I would think about what I did and smile at the thought of helping the cause of liberty, but that morning, I was just happy to be home in my bed.

* * *

"I lost many a night's sleep before that and would lose still more throughout the rest of the war," Sybil concluded, her voice having grown softer as she continued the story. "But I never expected that one such night would be spent riding through the woods in pouring rain to gather my father's regiment. I think that was the most satisfying sleepless night I ever had."

Henry's eyelids had been drooping for some time already, and as the story ended, he seemed to give up trying to keep them opening at all. Instead, he simply rolled onto his side, curling up as he nestled deeper into the warmth of the bed with a contented hum.

Edmund had been somewhat more attentive throughout but had also settled himself more comfortably. "Wow," he breathed, the word turning into a yawn he did not attempt to stifle. "I never thought of the war at people's homes like that."

"There's adventures and stories to be told in more places than you might think," Sybil replied, gently brushing a few strands of hair from his face. "Including in your dreams, so get some sleep now." She placed a kiss on each grandson's forehead before taking up the small candle holder—the candle burned low with wax dripping down into the tray—and quietly slipped out of the room.

Wrapped in Memories

Winter lays its shroud of frost upon the ground. Warm in the hearth fire's glow a family mourns Reuben, who fell from a hay mow. Harvest of the field, tucked safe away but at the cost of wounds that never healed. In the parlor, this husband, father, grandfather now does lay, dressed in his best, readied for the afterlife. His other attire, however worn it be from strife and toil, shall not go to waste. His grandchildren's scissors work with haste, cutting fabric; yellow, orange, and red they shape into diamonds, triangles, and squares for Esther. With her needle and thread, each shape is caught and a pattern she calls "tree of life" takes form. All the while three generations share stories of a beloved ancestor. From sorrow, bonds of love and care are built, from bits and shreds of cloth a patchwork quilt filled with memory.

Birdsong fills the spring morn as robins flit about, feathering their nests. Along the plains, a heavy laden wagon rolls toward the west. Within the wagon, Esther with her belly round, rests wrapped in the quilt. They leave behind leafy ferns and verdant memories for harsh climes where only the hardiest plants survive, yet she knows the patchwork leaves shall never wilt. Though she sees no traces, the wagon's path was paved with strife and guilt. Others, these routes did tread, who did not agree to leave their home, so the roots of families like hers could be spread and grown. Yet it is toward the future that her thoughts drift, to the life her coming babe will know. Fingers trace the tree of life, knowing challenges will be rife, and yet her loved ones look west to see manifest destiny. She wonders if a house will be built, expertly timed for the first child born in this western land, or if they'll first be swaddled cleverly in a wagon and quilt of memory.

The summer sun shines over fields of sheep, the dew-soaked grass and blooms perfume the air. *Surely, such a view could not be outdone by any city*, the matriarch thinks as she sits upon her son's bed. Yet the neatly laid quilt, worn and far from new, has stayed made for nights aplenty. Yet the letter in her hand bears news her boy, like the little meadowlark, has outgrown the nest. She watched him depart with an anxious heart as duty bade him go to trenches overseas, and how she did yearn for every letter. With every prayer, she spoke: God's will be done but please bring him home; trees need their roots and he would need his family close at hand. And when the war was won, sure enough, he sped across the sea until on the coast, he found a charming lass. The mother's every cautioning of distance and differing faith he did refute, his letters resolute. His heart knew better, for now in a New York chapel he is wed, a new life to be built with his wife. Though the apple may fall far, a family lives in the tree of life, stitched together securely as the quilt.

The air is cold and the ground is a blanket of color, yellow, orange, and red as I await the coming treasure. An heirloom that traveled too far to measure, across the land and finding its way back again today. Fittingly, the quilt with its tree should arrive upon Hudson's banks the day thanks are said by you and me. Stowed over years in boxes, basements, and closets without illumination for a generation, now to me an inheritance loved ones do bestow. My fingers trace the tree-like pattern, the fruits of someone's labor. A note: Esther Made Quilt 1865 for Reuben who fell from a hay mow. A "death quilt" in which life can still thrive and even grow. Threads of memory reaching across time, the stories that abound, so like the tree roots that spread beneath the ground. Small wonder to discover the design is what they call tree of life. Though leaves of the family tree did wilt and fall, memories of pride and shame, joy and pain, all that they overcame remain within this quilt.

All It Takes

Zoe lightly clasped her grandfather Zachary's calloused hand as they stood in the open lot. The two of them stood among a small crowd of people who had decided to come out despite the August heat. Most talked quietly together, while across the street construction workers prepared to move the Centennial Hose firehouse to its new home. They really were going to move a whole building! The nine-year-old thought the old building looked a little scary now, with the big opening in the front where the blue door used to be; the roof gone, revealing the metal beams; worn bricks and windows covered with sheets of metal. Still, it did have the two simple but pretty flowers decorating each end of what Grandpa called a frontispiece. Between the flowers the writing said, "4 CENTENNIAL 4," in gold letters, just above the gap that should have been where the fire trucks came in and out. Her dad had told her it would be just like when Grandpa worked there once they got it to its new home and repaired it to become a museum.

"Mommy said the firefighters from the memorial were from here," Zoe said, turning to look up at her grandpa, remembering the service they had gone to a few weeks ago.

"John Torpy and Walter Cole and the others were from Cortlandt Hook and Ladder Company," Zachary replied, glancing down at Zoe with warmth in his deep brown eyes. He gave his granddaughter's hand a little squeeze as he thought about the story that everyone from Centennial Hose Company knew so well. John Torpy had survived World War I and had recently returned to join Peekskill's volunteer fire department when the Fleischmann building caught fire; and Walter Cole was eighteen years old, it was his first and final major fire. "That was the ninetieth anniversary," Zachary added.

Zoe paused, biting at her lower lip as she tried to think about the numbers. "So…that was before the bridge made them take the roof away?" Zoe asked, pointing at Route 9 just above the old fire-house as a few cars sped along it.

"They only took the roof completely off for the move," Zachary explained, "but you're right. Back in the thirties, they had to take a little of the roof off so Route 9 could be built."

The old firehouse and Route 9 certainly had a history of tension, but in a way, Zachary was grateful for it this time. The building had practically been forgotten by the city of Peekskill. It had always felt as if few people other than Zachary and the other Dock Rats who had served in the riverside firehouse had even given the deteriorating old building a second glance. That was, until the Department of Transportation had condemned the building to be demolished to make way for its expansion of Route 9. Luckily, there had been enough people opposed to losing the historic building to convince the Department to work with the city and New York State Historic Preservation Office to arrange for the building to be moved and restored rather than destroyed.

"Is that why the roof leaked so much?" Zoe asked.

Zachary gave a wry smile at the memory of cold rain water seeping into his shoes and pant legs during every rainstorm. "I think it was more that the building was just old by that time," he told her. "That's why they moved us to the new building in 1980."

* * *

The sound of distant thunder could be heard from the firehouse as Zachary and a few of the other Dock Rats sat down at a small table with their lunches.

"Can't wait 'till we don't need to dread that sound," Tom commented as he set a plate of chicken salad on the table and dropped into the remaining empty seat. They had just heard the news that plans were being made to move the firehouse's headquarters to a new building. There would be some time before all the arrangements could be made, but Zachary gave an enthusiastic nod, his mouth currently full of a turkey sandwich as the other men made noises of agreement between bites of their own meals.

"Maybe the new place's heaters won't make such a racket," Zachary added when the nearby radiator began making a loud banging sound.

"No more yelling the bingo numbers just to be heard over that," Jonathan chuckled in response. "Speaking of; everyone still planning on a game tomorrow?"

The group cheerfully nodded or spoke up in agreement, all looking forward to the popular game.

* * *

There was a bittersweet look in Zachary's eyes as he turned his attention back to the firehouse. The memories of his days inside—there were all so vivid despite how many years had passed. It was only after they had actually made the move to new headquarters that he realized how much the weathered old bricks had made him feel connected to Centennial Hose's legacy. They still shared the stories of the firefighters that came before them in their new location, but the feeling of closeness, of imagining those brave men walking the same halls could only be found in the building before him. Not that he would complain, the new accommodation had been the most practical choice, and it did provide more convenience and comfort than the aging building ever could. But it was saddening to see the building being left to the mercy of vagrants as vines crept up its walls and the once bright red bricks began to crumble. The firehouse was almost like an old friend.

Once all the preparations had been made, the construction crew was ready to move the building. Zachary had read in the paper that they planned to move it about five hundred feet to the nearby parking lot for today. The whole move would take nearly ten months. As the faded brick structure rose from the ground, Zachary was glad they had decided to make the move slowly. The concept of moving an entire building any distance seemed amazing, taking into account that the building was 118 years old just made it all the more impressive. Even Zoe, who had been telling him about her day at the beach last week, fell silent as the two-story firehouse began to rotate so that it would be able to clear the power lines nearby before taking to the road.

The building turned in a slow, smooth movement and was now a few degrees from its original position. It was strange seeing a building move. So strange that just seeing it a few inches away from the position he was used to made it seem almost wrong—it almost looked like the walls were tilted. Quiet murmurs from the gathered people confirmed Zachary wasn't the only one to think so. It all seemed to happen too fast and painfully slow at the same time. The tilted look grew more extreme until the realization finally struck. It wasn't an illusion—the firehouse was tipping.

Zachary felt frozen as the shocked cries of the other witnesses mixed with the sound of brick cracking. Zachary just had time to register a few large fissures forming on the left side wall, and a puff of dust appearing behind the firehouse. The next thing he knew, the wall had completely broken apart and collapsed, taking the rest of the building with it. Zoe's nails dug into his skin as the crash echoed, and everyone stood in shock and a thick cloud of dust rose to hide the pile of rubble.

Zachary's heart pounded as the stunned silence gradually gave way to the voices of the spectators and the hurried questions and answers between the officials and the moving crew. After a moment of shock, Zachary's old instincts kicked in—there had been people standing near the building who could have been hurt. He had been retired for a long time now, but even if he was not as physically strong as he once was, his training and instinct to help had not faded with age. He was just about to step forward when a small, scared voice completely redirected his thoughts.

"Grandpa?" Zoe's eyes were wide and her small frame was trembling.

"Zoe, are you all right?" he asked, kneeling in front of her. Zoe's normally bright eyes were now wide and glassy as if she was trying hard to hold back tears.

"Y-yes, I guess. But it…your firehouse…why'd it…?" Her voice cracked a little before she trailed off. There were so many thoughts and questions running around in her head she couldn't even think how to get even one out. Just then someone announced that none of the moving crew was injured, but the words barely registered for Zoe as she watched her grandpa. He looked over at the person who made the announcement and his shoulders seemed to relax a little and then his eyes were back on her.

"I don't know," he said resting his hands on Zoe's shoulders. "They'll have to look through the remains to figure out what happened." Grandpa's voice sounded different as he said the last part. He sounded tired, and he glanced back at the big pile of bricks with a sad frown. Zoe sniffed, her hand hastily coming up to wipe at her eyes and nodded, not knowing what to say.

Zachary gave her shoulder a little squeeze, he wanted more than anything to comfort her, but his own mind was reeling with what had just happened, and any words he could think of just sounded hollow against the thoughts weighing on his own mind.

"It'll be awhile before they can do anything. How about I get you home?" he said, offering the only thing he could think of. Besides, it would probably do him some good to be away from the wreckage. Zoe nodded again, a tiny hiccupping sob escaping as she wiped her eyes again. Zachary took her small hand in his, guiding her back to where he had parked the car a few streets away. It was the first car ride with Zoe in years that the nine-year-old did not say a word. Her normal chatter was replaced by the weather and traffic reports coming from the radio, interrupted occasionally by a muffled sniffle or two from the backseat.

Zachary was just stepping out of the car after parking in the driveway when the front door opened and his daughter, Jane, appeared. "Wow, they moved the whole thing that fa—" Her smile faded as Zachary and Zoe approached. Her gaze, filled with worry as she took in Zoe's runny nose and the slight redness around her eyes. "Zoe, Sweetie, what's wrong?"

Zoe glanced down at the ground. She could hear that Mommy was worried, so she should tell her, but she didn't really want to answer. Her throat felt tight, and she had only just gotten the tears to stop trying to come out. If she tried to talk, it might break her concentration, and she'd really start to cry. She glanced down, fiddling with the end of her quarter-length sleeve and decided to just say it quick.

"The firehouse broke," she mumbled.

Mommy's head tilted a little, and she still had her worried frown, like maybe she had not heard Zoe's answer. Luckily, Grandpa spoke up instead.

"Something went wrong with the move," he said. "The whole building collapsed."

Mommy's eyes widened. "Wh... how..." she stammered out before taking a deep breath, just staring at Grandpa for a moment. "Are you all right?" she asked.

"Yeah, no one was hurt," Grandpa answered, rubbing the back of his neck.

"That's...good at least," Mommy replied, though she was frowning a little bit. "But...oh, Dad, I'm so sorry. And here I am keeping you two out on the lawn," she added, shaking her head and reaching out to hold Grandpa's arm and lead them toward the door.

They made their way into the kitchen where Mommy started to fill a teapot with water as Grandpa sat down in one of the chairs at the kitchen table. Zoe was still sad about the firehouse, but if Mommy was going to make tea it meant she was expecting a long talk. Zoe didn't want to talk about it anymore; it was only going to make her sadder. But she knew what would make her feel better.

"Mommy, can I go watch a movie?" she asked, coming to stand beside the sink.

Her mom turned looking at Zoe for a moment, like she was thinking about something. "Sure, sweetie," she replied after a moment, lightly brushing Zoe's bangs out of her eyes.

"Do me a favor first, though," Mommy whispered, leaning down toward her. "Give Grandpa a hug."

Zoe glanced over at her grandpa sitting at the kitchen table and looking out the window. She didn't like seeing him so sad. Mommy was right; he looked like he needed a hug. So she nodded and went over, wrapping her arms around him as she passed by. He seemed surprised at first, but then he wrapped an arm around her shoulders and squeezed back. After a moment, Zoe stepped back and went out to the hall. Before going to the living room, she hurried upstairs and scooped up her favorite teddy bear from her bed. Squeezing the bear tightly under her arm and then going to the big cabinet of DVDs to pick out a fun movie that would cheer her up.

Zachary and Jane settled at the kitchen table as he tried to explain what he could about what happened. But he had no idea what could have caused the collapse. The building's age seemed the easiest assumption; a case of overestimating what the long-neglected frame could take. Though he figured there could have been other possibilities—human error in the speed or degree of movement or perhaps just the machinery. Soon enough, they were talking about more typical subjects, though there was a noticeable somberness to the mood that was not normal for such casual talk between father and daughter. By the time, he took his last sip of tea though, Zachary simply felt like returning home. It had helped to talk with Jane, almost like thinking out loud but with the added benefit of a sympa-thetic ear and some of Jane's own thoughts. Even when they drifted away from the subject of the firehouse, it reminded him that it was just a building. No one had been hurt, and soon enough, everything would go back to normal. So he said his goodbyes to Jane and gave Zoe a kiss on the head where she sat watching some cartoon movie and made his way home.

* * *

"Can't believe the old stomping grounds are really gone," Tom's voice spoke through the phone. Tom was currently enjoying his retirement in Florida, but he still had family in the area who saw the collapse on the local news channel. Zachary had been getting quite a few calls from the men he had shared the building with as they got word of the collapse. There had been a few in the crowd at the time, but none who Zachary had been particularly close to, and for the most part, he had been too focused on Zoe to talk with them beyond casual hellos when they first arrived and certainly not when his granddaughter had been so upset after the collapse.

"I know what you mean," Zachary replied. "I saw it happen, and it still feels like it can't be real."

For all their complaints about the old place, being moved to the new headquarters all those years ago had been bittersweet as the sense of being separated from the Centennial Hose's history set in. Seeing the building collapse, reduced to little more than rubble, was an even harsher blow. As much as he missed the old place, before Zachary could not really say it hurt to be parted from it; he still passed it often enough, picking up a cake from the neighboring bakery every Saturday when his children and grandchildren came to visit as well as plenty of other outings around Peekskill. But now? Soon, the bricks would be cleaned up and all that would remain was an empty lot, or maybe they would replace it with a store or some other building.

"Did Danny mention if he was going to go to the memorial on Sunday?" he asked. Tom's only son having been the one to tell him about the collapse.

"I don't think so," Tom replied. "He mentioned it and asked if I'd want pictures or anything but..." there was a pause and Zachary could easily picture Tom giving the slight shrug he had used so often when talking about something and suddenly realized he was not sure how to explain it fully.

"I've got old pictures somewhere around from when we were still using the place. Em probably knows where they are—she's got some sorta system for all the pictures in those old boxes. Always finds stuff like that right off the bat even if I can't make hide nor hair of it," he added with a slight chuckle. "You planning on going?"

"Yeah, Jane and Ethan said they'd come too, and Zoe, 'course."

"You said Zoe was with you when it fell. How's she holding up?"

"She was pretty upset when it happened," Zachary replied. "But she's back to her old self now. You know how resilient kids are."

"Right, that's good." Tom replied. "Well, I gotta get going. Good talking to you, Zachary."

"You too, Tom. Say hi to Emily for me."

"Will do," Tom replied before Zachary hung up the phone.

* * *

As planned, Zachary and his family went to the memorial and afterward, came back to his house. He shared stories about his days working there, mostly his own personal memories, but he also found himself repeating stories that had been passed down from older firefighters to Zachary right inside those now crumbled walls.

"They really had horses pull the fire trucks?" Zoe asked, her hand hovering with a spoonful of chocolate ice cream and rainbow sprinkles. Hearing her favorite animal mentioned actually managing to distract her from the treat.

"Well, they didn't look exactly like the fire trucks you see driving around now," Zachary replied, smiling at his granddaughter's excitement. "Just like people rode around in carriages before the car came around, they had to get the water and firefighters to the fires somehow. So they used horse-drawn wagons. Before that, it was the firefighters who had to pull carts."

"Dragging around a big cart full of water?" Jane spoke up. "Talk about a workout, and that was before they even started fighting the fire. Yikes."

"I'm sure they were all pretty thrilled when they got enough money for the horses though," Zachary replied with a small laugh. "Seeing how happy the boys and I were to get away from a leaky roof, I can only imagine the relief of not having to pull the carts."

"I bet they fed the horses lots of sugar cubes!" Zoe piped up, after swallowing her spoonful of ice cream. "You're supposed to reward horses with sugar cubes, so it must have been how they thanked the horses for pulling the wagons."

This was met with cheerful laughter and comments of agreement. Zachary knew very little about horse care or how often they were supposed to be fed treats, but it was a nice thought.

"If we had a horse, it could take me to school," Zoe continued. "I'd let my friends take turns riding it, too. And then I'd give it a sugar cube every day!"

"And who would be cleaning out the stables?" her father asked teasingly.

"I would!" Zoe replied with obvious eagerness.

"Just like you clean your room, right, Zoe?" her mother added, suppressing a few giggles.

"Um…well," The nine-year-old's enthusiasm dimmed at that but only briefly. "I would for the horse. It would be fun spending more time around it."

To that, her mother simply gave a fond smile, shaking her head a little. Once dessert was finished, it was time for them to head home. And soon they had said their goodbyes, Zachary had the house to himself. It felt a bit odd, how easily things seemed to have returned to normal and yet at the same time, he still found small things that made him think of the old firehouse. Of course, the news reports served as reminders of what happened, often showing clips of the collapse, but with the memorial past, he doubted the news would be covering the story much longer. But for Zachary, reminders of his connection to the old place were still all around. Including the old photograph sitting on top of the television, showing him and the other Dock Rats during a little celebration they had put together after settling into the new headquarters. In his mind, he could still see their cars parked outside the two-story brick building and remember just where they liked to sit when they played bingo.

He still didn't particularly enjoy driving by the place where the firehouse had collapsed, but he didn't seek out other routes either. Funny how he thought he could sense the emptiness now when he had usually only given it a few moments of thought passing the building while it was still standing.

"That's my old firehouse," Zachary had told a five-year-old Zoe after picking her up from school. Jane had needed to go to a doctor's appointment and asked him to look after Zoe until it was finished. He glanced at the rearview mirror to see the little girl in her booster seat. She glanced up taking in the weathered brick structure.

"You drove the fire trucks, right, Grandpa?" she asked.

"Yup, right through that big blue door," he replied as the structure faded from sight.

"They should have made the doors pink," Zoe replied matter-of-factly. "It's almost red like the trucks, and pink's a pretty color."

Zachary had smiled, turning the corner to the next street and thoughts of the firehouse were soon replaced with plans of what to give Zoe for a snack when they got to the house and how much homework a kindergartener could possibly have.

Zachary knew he most likely had given the place and its history more thought than most people in Peekskill, but now he wondered if he should have given it more than just the occasional passing thought.

"Nothing to do about it now," he said, pulling open his dresser drawer and grabbing the first oversized shirt and pajama pants he saw. Occasionally, the memory of the smell of dust and sound of cracking brick came back to his mind, but he had to admit his days had slowly been returning to normal. And as for his family, they still listened to his reminiscing, but he suspected that their own thoughts were not turning to the firehouse nearly as often as his.

Soon the summer passed, and Zoe was back in school. The family's Saturday visits to Zachary's house were filled with her fondness for her new teacher, Miss Rodriguez, and the various games she and her friends invented at recess. The weeks passed with much the same routine as any other year. Zachary still felt a twinge of regret when he passed the firehouse's lot on his way to get cakes or cookies for the weekly visits but found that it passed quickly enough.

It was a Saturday in early November that caught Zachary by surprise, however. It began normally enough—Zoe bounding out of the car and up his driveway with the backpack she always used to carry her coloring books and toys for when the adult conversations became too boring for her. After they had settled into the living room and had exchanged some of the typical conversation topics, Jane turned to Zoe.

"Sweetie, why don't you tell Grandpa about your school project?" she prompted.

Zoe smiled brightly. She had practically been bouncing with excitement waiting for when she could tell Grandpa about the assignment. She reached into her backpack to pull out a spiral notebook, its solid pink cover adorned with sparkly stickers of various animals and the letters spelling "Social Studies" across the top. After a moment of flipping through the pages, she held the book open toward Zachary, revealing a drawing of a horse connected by a few lines to a large red box with wheels. An arrow pointed to the box with the word *water* written in blue crayon.

"It's the horses pulling the water wagon for the firefighters," Zoe explained. "Just like your firehouse used to use."

"Very nice," Zachary replied with an approving smile, though he was a bit confused about what this had to do with the school project Jane had mentioned. He found the answer to that when Zoe then took a sheet of paper out of the pocket on the inside of the notebook's cover and held it out to him.

"Miss Rodriquez says it's good to find something about history that we like so she wants everyone to do a presentation on something important to us."

The paper had a short paragraph about finding history with personal meaning followed by a list of suggestions, including, "The life of one of your family members," "Accomplishments of a famous person in the past," or "How your favorite sport started out." Looking over the list, Zachary noticed that various suggestions had been crossed out while others had small stars drawn next to them. The one that jumped out though was "An important piece of Peekskill's history," which was circled.

"For social studies, we have to teach each other about history," Zoe spoke up as Zachary continued to look over the assignment. "Miss Rodriguez said it could be something to do with our family or Peekskill or anything we like, so I wanna talk about your firehouse."

"Really?" Zachary replied a little surprised at her choice. Still, it was touching that she wanted to learn more about the firehouse. He had thought the nine-year-old would have completely forgotten it by now, but instead, she was actually planning to learn and tell others more about it. Out of everything she could have chosen, he was surprised, albeit pleasantly, that she would come up with that idea herself.

"Yeah," Zoe replied. "I liked all your stories about when you were there, and I figured everybody else in my class might like them, too. Do you think you can tell me more stories about it?"

"Sure," Zachary replied, reaching an arm across Zoe's shoulders and giving a gentle squeeze. "I've even got some pictures in the attic if you want to use them in your presentation," he suggested.

"Really?" Zoe asked, her face alight with a bright smile. "That'd be really cool." Her smile faltered, however, as she remembered the glimpses she had gotten of Grandpa's attic when he asked Daddy to get some things down for him. It was really dark up there, with stacks of old boxes and a low roof that she could see the beams of. "I don't have to go into the attic, though, do I?"

Daddy chuckled. "If your grandpa needs any help getting them, I can take care of that," he reassured her.

"Okay," Zoe replied, her smile returning now that her fears about going in the dark and scary attic were set aside.

"I'm still picking you up from school on Tuesday, right?" Zachary asked. Zoe's school had a half-day and neither of her parents could get off from work so they had planned on Zoe spending the afternoon at Zachary's. "I'll have some of them down by then, and we can take a look."

"Okay!" Zoe replied enthusiastically. She cheerfully showed Zachary the rest of her notebook. It was mostly drawings of some of the details Zachary had already told her and one of what the firehouse looked like just before the move. There were a few notes explaining the drawings or captions mentioning facts she had recalled. Zachary could not help but smile listening to Zoe proudly repeat the anecdotes he had shared. He had been wondering if the firehouse might just fade from memory again, and this time, with nothing left to remind anyone later. But listening to his granddaughter repeat his stories, he felt a new hope that maybe all the history those old bricks carried was not completely lost after all.

About the Author

Lindsey Wood grew up in the Hudson Valley where she developed a love of history at an early age. She graduated from Wells College with a BA in history and entered the museum profession as a tour guide at Historic Hudson Valley. She continued on toward a Master's in museum studies with Johns Hopkins University. Lindsey has been especially fascinated with the everyday lives of people of the past and draws inspiration for her stories and poems from museum collections and her own experience as a historical reenactor. Her volunteer work includes serving as a director and social media manager for Van Cortlandtville Historical Society and is on the board of Friends of Odell House Rochambeau Headquarters, supporting their efforts to restore and open the historic house to the public. Lindsey now spends her days living a childhood dream of dressing up in eighteenth-century clothes while spinning wool or working over a hearth in historic houses.

CPSIA information can be obtained
at www.ICGtesting.com
Printed in the USA
LVHW111554020821
694315LV00015B/209

9 781662 442353